TEENS WHO THRIVE: 12 SUCCESS STORIES

REAL STORIES OF TEENS WITH ADHD INCLUDING PROVEN STRATEGIES, REFLECTION EXERCISES, AND WEEKLY ACTION PLANS TO HELP YOU THRIVE TOO

RICHARD BASS

Copyright Page

Teens Who Thrive: 12 Success Stories

Copyright © 2026 by Richard Bass

All rights reserved. No part of this book may be reproduced or transmitted in any form or by any means, electronic or mechanical, including photocopying, recording, or by any information storage and retrieval system, without written permission from the author, except for the inclusion of brief quotations in a review.

Published by RBG Publishing

First Edition: 2026

Disclaimer: This book is designed to provide information and motivation to readers. It is sold with the understanding that the author and publisher are not engaged to render any type of psychological, medical, legal, or any other kind of professional advice. The content is the sole expression and opinion of the author. No warranties or guarantees are expressed or implied by the choice to include any of the content in this book. Neither the publisher nor the author shall be liable for any physical, psychological, emotional, financial, or commercial damages, including but not limited to special, incidental, consequential, or other damages. You are responsible for your own choices, actions, and results.

The characters and stories in this book are fictional composites created for educational purposes. While they reflect common ADHD experiences and evidence-based strategies, they do not represent any specific individuals.

Medical Disclaimer

Important Notice to Readers

This book is intended for educational and informational purposes only. It is not intended to diagnose, treat, cure, or prevent any medical or psychological condition, including ADHD (Attention-Deficit/Hyperactivity Disorder).

Please note:

- The stories in this book are fictional composites designed to illustrate common ADHD challenges and evidence-based strategies. They are not substitutes for professional medical or mental health advice.
- If you suspect you or your teen has ADHD, please seek evaluation from a qualified healthcare provider, such as a pediatrician, psychiatrist, psychologist, or licensed mental health professional.
- The strategies discussed in this book are based on research and clinical best practices, but individual results may vary. What works for one person with ADHD may not work for another.
- Medication decisions should always be made in consultation with a

qualified healthcare provider who knows your individual medical history
and needs.
- If you or your teen is experiencing a mental health crisis, please contact a
mental health professional, call 988 (Suicide and Crisis Lifeline), or go to
your nearest emergency room.
- The information in this book is current as of the publication date. ADHD
research and treatment approaches continue to evolve. Always consult with
healthcare professionals for the most current information.

This book is meant to complement, not replace, the relationship you have with healthcare providers and mental health professionals.

DEDICATION

For every teen who's been told they're "not trying hard enough"
You are trying. So hard it's exhausting.
Your brain just works differently, and that's not a flaw.
This book is for you.

For the parents, teachers, and professionals who see beyond the symptoms to
the capable, creative, resilient humans underneath
Thank you for understanding that different doesn't mean less.

And for my own child, who inspires me every day to build a world that
celebrates all kinds of minds.

I wrote this book because I wish it had existed when I was working with teens struggling to understand their ADHD.

As a special education teacher and author specializing in neurodivergent support, I've spent over a decade listening to teens describe their ADHD experiences. What struck me most was the pattern: almost every teen saw ADHD only as a list of deficits. Things they couldn't do. Ways they were broken. Accommodations they needed because they weren't "normal."

Very few had been taught that ADHD comes with both challenges and strengths. That their brains work differently, not wrongly. That success doesn't mean becoming neurotypical it means building systems that work for how their brains actually function.

This book grew from those conversations. The twelve stories you'll read are fictional, but they're built from real experiences, real struggles, and real breakthroughs I've witnessed in classrooms, counseling sessions, and conversations with teens navigating ADHD.

Each story addresses a different aspect of ADHD: executive function challenges, emotional dysregulation, rejection sensitivity, impulsivity, hyperactivity, working memory deficits, and more. But more importantly, each story shows that understanding your brain and building the right supports makes thriving possible.

The Reflect sections ask questions to help you see yourself in these stories. The Act sections provide concrete, evidence-based strategies you can implement immediately. These aren't theoretical they're tools that actually work when consistently applied.

If you're a teen with ADHD reading this: You're not broken. You're not lazy. You're not "too much" or "not enough." Your brain is wired differently, and with the right understanding and tools, you can absolutely thrive.

If you're a parent reading this: Your teen is trying. The struggles are real, the exhaustion is real, and so is their potential. Understanding ADHD really understanding it changes everything.

Let's begin.

Richard Bass

This book is designed to be both read and used you'll find stories, insights, and actionable strategies throughout.

The Structure

Each chapter follows the same format:

THE STORY: A realistic narrative about a teen with ADHD facing a specific challenge. These stories are fictional but based on real experiences and research. You'll likely see yourself in many of these characters.

REFLECT: Eight questions to help you think about your own experiences. These aren't tests there are no right or wrong answers. They're designed to help you recognize patterns in your own life and understand your ADHD better.

ACT: One focused action plan you can implement this week. These strategies are evidence-based and specifically designed for ADHD brains. You don't have to do every action in every chapter pick the ones that resonate most with your specific challenges.

How to Read This Book

If you're a teen with ADHD:

- You don't have to read the stories in order. Scan the Table of Contents and start with whichever challenge feels most pressing for you right now.
- Read the story first to see the strategy in action, then use the Reflect section to think about your own experience.
- Pick ONE Act strategy to try this week. Don't try to implement everything at once that's overwhelming and sets you up for failure.
- Come back to chapters as you're ready. This book is a resource you can return to whenever you face a particular challenge.
- Share chapters with parents, teachers, or counselors if you want them to understand what you're experiencing.

If you're a parent:

- Read the stories to understand what your teen might be experiencing internally, even if they can't articulate it.

- The strategies in the Act sections can guide how you support your teen but remember, they need to be the ones implementing the strategies. You can't do this for them.
- Don't force your teen to read this book or complete every exercise. Let them engage with it in their own time and way.
- The Reflect questions can spark valuable conversations if your teen is willing to discuss them.

If you're an educator or professional:

- These stories can help you understand the internal experience of ADHD beyond what you see in the classroom.
- The Act sections provide concrete strategies you can suggest or accommodate in your setting.
- Consider recommending specific chapters to students facing particular challenges.

A Note on Strategies

The Act sections provide evidence-based strategies, but not every strategy works for every person. ADHD is highly individual. If a strategy doesn't work for you after genuinely trying it, that's okay move on to the next one. The goal is to build a toolkit of strategies that work for YOUR brain, not to follow a one-size-fits-all prescription.

You Don't Have to Do This Alone

The teens in these stories often work with parents, counselors, doctors, and other professionals. That's realistic. Managing ADHD isn't about rugged individualism it's about building the right supports. If you don't have professional support and need it, the Resources section at the back of this book can help you find it.

Most Importantly

These stories all have one thing in common: the teens learn that ADHD doesn't mean they're broken. It means they're different. And different, with the right understanding and tools, can absolutely thrive.

Let's get started.

INTRODUCTION: YOU'RE NOT BROKEN

Let's start with what you probably already know:

Having ADHD in high school is hard.

You might read a paragraph five times and still have no idea what it said. You might spend six hours on homework that should take two. You might forget test dates despite writing them down. You might interrupt people even when you're trying desperately not to. You might lose things constantly your keys, your assignments, your train of thought mid-sentence.

And here's what makes it even harder: most people don't get it.

They see you struggling and think: *If they just tried harder. If they just paid attention. If they just cared more. If they just got organized. If they just stopped being so dramatic/lazy/careless/irresponsible.*

But here's what they don't see:

You ARE trying. You're trying so hard it's exhausting. You're using every ounce of mental energy just to keep up with what seems effortless for everyone else. You're not lazy you're working three times harder than your neurotypical peers for the same results.

You ARE paying attention. You're listening so intently your brain hurts. But the information slides right through your working memory like water through a sieve. It's not that you weren't listening. It's that your brain didn't store what you heard.

You DO care. Probably more than most people. Your ADHD brain feels everything intensely including the frustration of wanting desperately to succeed and not knowing why it's so much harder for you than for everyone else.

The problem isn't you. The problem is that your brain works differently, and most of the world including most schools is designed for brains that work another way.

What ADHD Actually Is

Let's clear up some misconceptions right away.

ADHD is not:

- Laziness
- Lack of discipline
- Bad parenting
- Too much screen time
- An excuse for bad behavior
- Something you'll "grow out of"
- Something you can overcome with more willpower

ADHD is a neurodevelopmental condition. That means your brain is wired differently from neurotypical brains. It's not broken it's different. And that difference comes with both challenges and strengths (yes, really we'll get to that).

The science part (simplified): ADHD affects the prefrontal cortex the part of your brain responsible for executive functions like focus, impulse control, working memory, emotional regulation, time management, and task initiation. It also affects how your brain produces and processes neurotransmitters like dopamine and norepinephrine.

What that actually means: Your brain isn't lazy or undisciplined. It literally processes information, regulates attention, manages time, controls impulses, and handles emotions differently than neurotypical brains. The struggles you experience aren't character flaws they're neurological differences.

The Three Types (And Why Labels Matter Less Than You Think)

ADHD has three main presentations:

ADHD-Inattentive: Primarily difficulties with focus, attention, and working memory. Often called "invisible ADHD" because the struggles are internal and easily missed or dismissed as laziness.

ADHD-Hyperactive/Impulsive: Primarily difficulties with physical restlessness and impulse control. The most visible type, but often misunderstood as misbehavior rather than neurological difference.

ADHD-Combined: Both inattentive and hyperactive/impulsive traits.

Here's the thing though: ADHD is more complex than these three categories suggest. You might have combined type but struggle most with emotional regulation. You might have inattentive type but also deal with rejection sensitivity. Labels are useful for diagnosis and accommodations, but they don't capture the full picture of YOUR specific ADHD experience.

That's why this book focuses on specific challenges executive function, emotional dysregulation, working memory, impulsivity, etc. rather than types. You'll find yourself in multiple stories, regardless of your official diagnosis.

What Makes ADHD So Hard (And Why People Don't Get It)

Here's what makes ADHD particularly challenging:

It's inconsistent. You can hyperfocus for six hours on something you love, but you can't focus for six minutes on something boring. People see the hyperfocus and think, "See? You CAN focus when you want to!" They don't understand that ADHD isn't about can't focus ever it's about can't control where your focus goes.

It's invisible. Broken bones get casts. Vision problems get glasses. But ADHD struggles happen inside your brain where nobody can see them. So people assume you're choosing not to try, not that you're battling neurological barriers.

It's variable. Some days your ADHD is manageable. Other days it's overwhelming. This inconsistency makes people think you're not trying on bad days, when really your ADHD symptoms fluctuate based on sleep, stress, stimulation level, and factors you can't always control.

It's complex. ADHD affects so many different brain functions that it creates cascading challenges. Executive dysfunction affects organization, which affects homework completion, which affects grades, which affects self-esteem, which affects motivation, which makes executive dysfunction worse. It's not one simple problem to solve.

It's lifelong. You don't grow out of ADHD. Your brain remains wired differently. But and this is crucial you can learn to work WITH your brain instead of against it. That's what this book is about.

The Thing Nobody Tells You (But Should)

Here's what most ADHD resources focus on: problems. Deficits. Challenges. Things you can't do. Ways you're struggling.

And yes, those are real. This book doesn't sugarcoat the challenges. But here's what gets left out of most conversations about ADHD:

ADHD comes with strengths.

Real, genuine, valuable strengths that are part of how your brain is wired.

ADHD brains often excel at:

- Creative thinking and making unusual connections
- Hyperfocusing on engaging work and producing exceptional results
- Thinking quickly and adapting in crisis or novel situations
- Bringing high energy and enthusiasm to interests
- Seeing patterns across different contexts
- Taking risks and trying unconventional approaches
- Feeling emotions including joy, passion, and love with full intensity

These aren't compensations for the challenges. They're part of what ADHD is. The same brain wiring that makes traditional school difficult can make creative work easier. The same impulsivity that gets you in trouble can make you brave enough to try things others won't. The same distractibility that hurts in lectures can help you notice details and connections others miss.

The problem is that most environments especially schools are designed to punish ADHD weaknesses and ignore ADHD strengths. You're constantly being measured against neurotypical standards in neurotypical environments. That doesn't mean you're less capable. It means you're being judged by the wrong rubric.

What This Book Will (And Won't) Do
This book will:

- Show you that you're not alone in your struggles
- Help you understand WHY ADHD makes certain things so hard
- Provide concrete, evidence-based strategies that actually work for ADHD brains
- Help you recognize your strengths alongside your challenges
- Teach you to advocate for accommodations and supports you need
- Guide you toward building systems that work for YOUR brain instead of forcing yourself to work like neurotypical brains

This book won't:

- Claim ADHD is all positive (it's not the challenges are real)
- Suggest you can "overcome" ADHD with enough willpower (you can't it's neurological)
- Provide a one-size-fits-all solution (ADHD is highly individual)
- Replace professional support (therapy, medication, accommodations are often necessary)
- Make ADHD disappear (you'll always have ADHD; the goal is learning to work with it)

How These Stories Work

Each of the twelve chapters tells the story of a teen with ADHD facing a specific challenge:

Tyler deals with ADHD-Inattentive that was masked by high intelligence until demands exceeded his ability to compensate. Zara struggles with time blindness and feeling like everything takes her longer than everyone else. Mason battles hyperfocus that's both superpower and curse. Jasmine experiences emotional dysregulation that others call "too sensitive." Jordan faces Rejection Sensitive Dysphoria that makes perceived rejection feel devastating.

And seven more stories covering medication decisions, organization struggles, impulsivity, hyperactivity, prioritization challenges, working memory deficits, and recognizing ADHD strengths.

These stories are fictional, but they're built from real experiences. As a special education teacher and author specializing in ADHD support, I've worked with hundreds of teens navigating these exact challenges. Every story reflects real struggles, real breakthroughs, and real strategies that work.

After each story, you'll find:

REFLECT: Questions to help you see yourself in the story and understand your own ADHD patterns.

ACT: One concrete strategy you can implement this week to address that specific challenge.

You don't have to read every story or implement every strategy. Pick what resonates. Build your own toolkit.

The Most Important Thing to Understand

Your ADHD brain isn't a broken neurotypical brain. It's a different kind of brain with different strengths and different challenges.

Success doesn't mean becoming neurotypical. It means:

- Understanding how YOUR brain specifically works
- Building systems and strategies that work FOR your brain, not against it
- Getting accommodations and supports for your challenges
- Finding environments where your strengths matter
- Accepting that you'll always need different tools than neurotypical people and that's okay

The teens in these stories don't "overcome" their ADHD. They learn to understand it, work with it, advocate for what they need, and build lives where they can thrive.

You can do the same.

A Note to Parents Reading This

If you're a parent reading this introduction, a few things:

Your teen IS trying. When they forget things, lose things, miss deadlines, struggle to start tasks they're not being defiant or lazy. They're battling neurological barriers you can't see.

The best thing you can do is believe them when they say something is hard. Even if it seems easy. Even if neurotypical kids can do it. Even if they could do it yesterday but can't today. ADHD makes things genuinely difficult in ways that aren't visible.

You can't fix this with more consequences or more rewards. ADHD isn't a motivation problem. It's a brain wiring difference that needs accommodation, strategy, and often professional support.

Your role is to help them build supports, advocate for accommodations, provide structure they can't create alone, and remind them constantly that they're not broken.

This book can help you understand what your teen experiences internally. It can guide conversations about challenges and strategies. But ultimately, your teen has to be the one implementing the strategies. You can support, but you can't do it for them.

Let's Begin

Somewhere in these twelve stories, you'll find yourself. You'll see your struggles reflected back and realize: I'm not the only one. I'm not broken. I'm not lazy. My brain just works differently.

And you'll learn that different with the right understanding, tools, and supports can absolutely thrive.

Let's start with Tyler's story.

STORY 1: THE INVISIBLE STRUGGLE

A STORY about learning that high intelligence can mask ADHD until demands exceed your capacity to compensate and struggling invisibly doesn't mean you're lazy, it means you need external systems and support.

Tyler Chen stared at the same sentence for the fourth time. *The Missouri Compromise of 1820 was a significant legislative agreement that...* The words blurred together like watercolors in rain. He blinked hard, pressed his fingers against his temples, and tried again.

It was 10:17 AM on a Tuesday. AP US History. His favorite class. Mr. Patterson was explaining the causes of the Civil War at the front of the room something Tyler actually cared about, something he'd spent hours listening to podcasts about. But his mind kept sliding sideways.

Did I text Alex back about debate practice? Wait, what's that assignment due in Chem? Is that girl in the third row wearing the same shirt as yesterday or do I just not pay attention? Focus. FOCUS. Okay, Missouri Compromise. Missouri... compromise... what did I just read?

His phone buzzed in his pocket. He pulled it out under his desk.

Mom: *How was the history test?* 🙂

Tyler's stomach dropped like an elevator with cut cables.

The test. The test was *today*?

He pulled up the syllabus on his laptop with shaking hands. There it was. **Chapter 12-14 Exam: October 17th.** Today. He'd studied chapters 9-11. He'd written "test next week" in his planner. He'd been *so sure* it was next week.

"Tyler?" Mr. Patterson's voice cut through the fog. "Care to share your thoughts on the Compromise's impact on sectional tensions?"

Twenty-eight faces turned toward him. Tyler's mind went blank.

"I... uh..." The answer was in there somewhere. He'd read about this. He knew this. Why couldn't he find it? "I think... it made things worse? Because... um..."

"Because it temporarily resolved the slavery expansion question while embedding deeper contradictions into the system," Mr. Patterson finished gently. "Maybe review chapters 12-14 before the test this afternoon."

Laughter rippled through the room. Tyler's face burned.

He'd been the "smart kid" his entire life. Elementary school was easy straight A's without trying. Middle school was a breeze. Even freshman and sophomore year were manageable. Sure, he had to work a little harder than some kids, but nothing major.

Junior year was different.

Junior year was drowning.

That night, Tyler sat at his desk at 4:00 PM with a color-coded study plan and three textbooks. He had two essays due Friday, a calculus problem set due tomorrow, chemistry lab write-up, and he needed to prep evidence cards for Saturday's debate tournament. Totally doable. Five hours of focused work, he'd be fine.

At 4:47 PM, he realized he'd been staring at his laptop screen, having absorbed exactly nothing from the AP Lang essay prompt.

Come on. Just START. Write one sentence.

He wrote: "In the novel To Kill a Mockingbird, Harper Lee explores themes of "

What were the themes again? He'd read the book. He'd taken notes. Where were his notes? He opened three different notebooks, two Google Docs, checked his phone photos. Found them. Okay. Racial injustice, moral growth, perspective-taking.

He returned to the document. What had he already written? He reread his one sentence. Right. Themes.

His phone buzzed. Alex: *You coming to debate practice or what?*

Debate practice. That was today? He checked the calendar. Yes. 6 PM. But if he went to debate practice, when would he finish homework? He texted back: *Can't. Drowning in work.*

At 6:15 PM, his mom called him down for dinner.

"I can't," Tyler called from his room. "Too much homework."

"You need to eat, honey."

"I'll eat later."

At 7:30 PM, he was on page three of a fifteen-page reading assignment for history. Not because the reading was difficult he understood every word. But every paragraph required three, four, five reads before anything stuck. It was like trying to pour water into a colander.

At 9:00 PM, his dad knocked on the door. "Bedtime soon, bud. You've been at it for five hours."

Five hours. Tyler looked at his planner. He'd completed maybe 30% of what he'd meant to finish.

"I'm not done yet."

"You need sleep. Just finish it in the morning."

"I can't finish five hours of work in one morning, Dad."

His father frowned. "Well, maybe you need to manage your time better. Less debate, more focus on academics."

Tyler wanted to scream. He'd been sitting at his desk for *five hours straight*. How was that not focused?

After his dad left, Tyler kept working. At 11:00 PM, his eyes burned. At 1:00 AM, he was still going. At 2:30 AM, he finally crawled into bed with three things unfinished, his mind racing with everything he'd failed to do.

He lay there for another hour, his brain refusing to shut off, rehearsing tomorrow's disaster, before finally falling into anxious, shallow sleep.

This pattern continued for weeks. The harder Tyler tried, the worse things got.

He tried studying in the library. Same problem the words wouldn't stick.

He tried the Pomodoro Technique he'd read about online. Twenty-five minutes on, five minutes off. It worked for two days before he started "taking breaks" that lasted forty minutes and work sessions that involved twenty minutes of staring at the wall.

He tried putting his phone in another room. Didn't matter. His own brain was distraction enough.

His grades were slipping. His first B ever in English. A C in AP Chemistry. His parents were "concerned." No they were disappointed.

"What's going on with you?" his mom asked over dinner one night. "You used to get straight A's without even trying."

"I'm trying really hard, Mom."

"Well, you need to try harder. Your sister never struggled like this."

His sister Michelle. Perfect Michelle, currently crushing medical school, who'd been valedictorian, who'd never gotten below an A- in her life. The unspoken comparison hung in the air constantly.

"Maybe he's spending too much time on debate," his dad offered.

"I'm not"

"You need to prioritize, son. Debate isn't going to get you into college. Grades will."

Tyler bit his tongue. He'd been on debate team since freshman year. He was co-captain. It was the one place he felt genuinely good at something. And honestly, it was the only thing keeping him sane.

But maybe they were right. Maybe he needed to quit everything and just focus.

So he did. He quit debate team. He stopped seeing friends. He came straight home after school every day and worked until midnight, sometimes later.

His grades improved slightly. The C became a B-. The B's stayed B's.

But Tyler felt hollowed out. Empty. Like he'd given up everything and was still failing.

The breaking point came at the State Debate Tournament in early November.

Tyler had rejoined the team after three weeks Ms. Rodriguez, the coach, had texted him repeatedly asking him to come back, saying they needed him. He'd finally caved, telling himself he could balance both. He'd prepared his evidence, practiced his arguments, felt as ready as possible.

He and Alex were in the semifinal round. Affirmative case on criminal justice reform. Tyler knew this topic inside and out. He'd spent hours researching recidivism rates, rehabilitation programs, sentencing disparities.

But when he stood up for his rebuttal speech, his mind went blank.

He looked down at his evidence cards. The words swam. What was his argument again? Something about... rehabilitation? No, wait, that was the other team's point. His was about... sentencing? Mass incarceration?

Alex was staring at him, waiting. The judge was waiting. The opposing team looked confused.

Tyler's hands started shaking. His throat closed up. He couldn't remember. He couldn't *remember*. He'd spent fifteen hours preparing and he couldn't remember a single coherent argument.

"I... the, um... the statistics show that..." He shuffled through his evidence cards desperately. "Mass incarceration creates... um..."

Alex jumped in, thank god. "What my partner is emphasizing is that rehabilitative programs reduce recidivism by 43%, as shown by our Johnson 2019 evidence..." She took over the entire speech.

They lost. Badly.

Afterward, the team gathered in the school lobby waiting for parents to pick them up. Most of the other debaters were rehashing their rounds, but Tyler sat apart, staring at his phone.

Ms. Rodriguez sat down next to him. "You want to talk about what happened up there?"

Tyler shook his head.

"Tyler, I've coached you for two years. That wasn't nerves. That was something else." She paused. "What's going on? And please don't say 'nothing.'"

Maybe it was because he was too exhausted to keep pretending. Maybe it was because she was one of the few adults who'd never made him feel stupid. But Tyler told her. Everything. The focus problems that were getting worse. The memory issues forgetting test dates, losing track of assignments even when he wrote them down, reading paragraphs over and over. The exhaustion. The feeling like his brain was wrapped in cotton. The way he could spend six hours on homework that should take two. The constant fear that he was lazy, that he wasn't smart enough, that everyone was finally seeing through him.

Ms. Rodriguez listened without interrupting. When he finished, she was quiet for a moment.

Then she said, "Tyler, have you ever been evaluated for ADHD?"

Tyler almost laughed. "ADHD? I'm not hyperactive. I can sit still for hours. I hyperfocus on things I'm interested in. I just... need to try harder."

"ADHD isn't always hyperactivity," Ms. Rodriguez said gently. "There's a type called inattentive ADHD. No hyperactivity at all. It looks exactly like what you're describing difficulty sustaining attention, forgetfulness, mental fog, reading without retaining information."

"But I'm smart. I've always been a good student."

"Exactly. That's why it can go undiagnosed for years. Smart kids compensate. They work twice as hard as everyone else and get average results, and everyone assumes they're just not trying." She paused. "I have ADHD. Inattentive type. I wasn't diagnosed until college, after I had a breakdown similar to what you experienced today."

Tyler stared at her. Ms. Rodriguez was one of the most organized, capable adults he knew.

She pulled out her phone and showed him an article. "Just read this. See if it resonates."

That night, Tyler read the article. Then five more. Then took three different ADHD screening questionnaires online.

Every symptom list read like his autobiography:

- Difficulty sustaining attention in tasks ✓
- Doesn't seem to listen when spoken to directly ✓
- Fails to finish schoolwork or tasks ✓
- Difficulty organizing tasks and activities ✓
- Avoids or dislikes tasks requiring sustained mental effort ✓
- Loses things necessary for tasks ✓
- Easily distracted by extraneous stimuli ✓
- Forgetful in daily activities ✓

The screening questionnaires all said the same thing: "High likelihood of ADHD. Seek professional evaluation."

Tyler felt something crack open in his chest. Relief? Terror? Hope?

Maybe he wasn't lazy. Maybe he wasn't stupid. Maybe his brain just worked differently.

But telling his parents was going to be a disaster.

He was right.

"Everyone has trouble focusing sometimes," his mom said when he brought it up at dinner the next night. "You're just stressed. Junior year is hard for everyone."

"But Mom, I took these screening tests and "

"Those online tests aren't real diagnoses, Tyler. They're designed to make you think something's wrong so you'll buy something."

"It's not like that. Ms. Rodriguez said "

"Your debate coach is not a doctor," his dad interrupted. "Look, I get that school is hard right now. But ADHD is way overdiagnosed. Every kid who doesn't want to do homework claims they have ADHD these days."

"I'm not making this up! I've been "

"You don't need medication," his mom said firmly. "You need better study habits. You need to put your phone away and eliminate distractions."

"My phone is in another room when I study!"

"Then you need more discipline. More structure."

Tyler felt tears burning behind his eyes. He stood up. "Forget it."

He went upstairs and slammed his door something he hadn't done since he was twelve. His parents didn't understand. They thought he was looking for excuses. They thought ADHD was fake, or exaggerated, or something only "bad kids" had.

For the next two weeks, Tyler tried even harder to "fix" himself through pure willpower. He color-coded his notes. He made elaborate study schedules. He set seventeen phone alarms. He tried studying standing up, sitting down, lying on the floor. He did jumping jacks between study sessions to "wake up his brain."

Nothing worked. His grades continued falling. He had a full-blown panic attack before his AP Calc test, hyperventilating in the bathroom.

His school counselor, Mr. Barnes, noticed. He called Tyler in for a "check-in."

"I'm fine," Tyler said automatically.

"You had a panic attack before a test. That's not fine."

Tyler broke. He told Mr. Barnes everything the focus problems, the suspicion about ADHD, his parents' refusal to take him seriously.

Mr. Barnes nodded thoughtfully. "Would you be comfortable if I called your parents in for a meeting? Sometimes parents need to hear concerns from school staff."

Tyler agreed, though he wasn't hopeful.

The meeting happened three days later. Tyler, his parents, and Mr. Barnes sat in the counselor's office.

Mr. Barnes was diplomatic but firm. "I've been a school counselor for eighteen years. I've worked with hundreds of students with ADHD. Tyler's presentation is textbook inattentive ADHD and the fact that he's made it to junior year with good grades actually supports that diagnosis. Bright kids compensate for years before the demands exceed their capacity to cope."

"But he's never had these problems before," Tyler's mom protested.

"Because the demands weren't high enough before. Four AP classes with executive function challenges? That's like asking someone to run a marathon with a broken leg and wondering why they're struggling."

"So you think he needs to be medicated," his dad said flatly.

"I think he needs to be *evaluated*. By a professional. Who can determine what support he needs which may or may not include medication, but definitely includes accommodations and strategies."

His parents were silent.

"At minimum," Mr. Barnes continued, "let's rule it out. If he gets evaluated and doesn't have ADHD, great. But if he does have it and we don't address it, we're setting him up for continued struggle."

Finally, reluctantly, his parents agreed to an evaluation.

The evaluation process took three weeks. Questionnaires for Tyler, his parents, his teachers. An appointment with Dr. Okonkwo, a psychologist who specialized in ADHD. Interviews about his developmental history, his current struggles, his coping strategies. Some cognitive testing.

Tyler was terrified. What if he didn't have ADHD? What if he was just lazy, and now he'd wasted everyone's time and money proving it?

The results appointment was on a Friday in December. Tyler, his parents, and Dr. Okonkwo sat in her office.

"Based on the comprehensive evaluation," Dr. Okonkwo said, "Tyler meets criteria for ADHD, Predominantly Inattentive Presentation. Moderate to severe."

Tyler felt dizzy. Relief and vindication crashed through him.

It's real. I'm not lazy. I'm not stupid.

His mom was crying. "I don't... I don't understand. He's always been such a good kid."

"ADHD has nothing to do with being 'good' or 'bad,'" Dr. Okonkwo said gently. "It's a neurological condition affecting executive function the brain's management system. Tyler's high intelligence has masked it for years. He's been compensating through sheer cognitive horsepower. But junior year exceeded his compensation capacity."

"So what does this mean?" his dad asked. He looked shaken.

"It means Tyler has been working approximately ten times harder than his peers to get the same results. It means he's not lazy he's exhausted. And it means we can help."

Dr. Okonkwo explained treatment options: behavioral strategies, academic accommodations, possibly medication. She recommended Tyler work with the school to get formal accommodations extended time on tests, access to recorded lectures, copies of notes, permission to use fidget tools.

"And medication?" his mom asked quietly.

"That's a family decision. Stimulant medications are very effective for ADHD they help the executive function system work more efficiently. But they're not the only option, and they're not required."

Tyler spoke up for the first time. "I want to try."

His parents exchanged glances.

"Let's talk to your pediatrician," his mom finally said.

The next two months were a process of trial and adjustment.

Tyler met with Mr. Barnes to set up accommodations: extended time on tests (time-and-a-half), access to teacher study guides, permission to record lectures, seating at the front of the classroom, ability to use fidgets or take movement breaks.

He started implementing systems that worked *with* his ADHD instead of against it:

- Everything went into his phone calendar with three reminder alerts

- A giant whiteboard on his wall with visual checklists
- Sunday night planning sessions became non-negotiable
- Pomodoro technique, but with physical movement breaks
- Body doubling studying at the library with friends, even when working on different subjects

He also started medication. Low dose of a stimulant. His pediatrician monitored closely for side effects.

The first day he took it, Tyler sat in the library and cried.

He read three pages of his history textbook and *remembered what he read*. He completed a homework assignment in forty-five minutes the amount of time it was supposed to take. The constant mental fog lifted. His thoughts felt... clear. Organized. Like someone had cleaned the windshield he'd been trying to see through.

When his mom picked him up from school, she asked nervously, "How do you feel? Any side effects?"

Tyler turned to her. "I feel like everyone else must feel all the time."

She started crying.

It wasn't magic. Medication helped, but it didn't fix everything. He still needed accommodations. He still needed systems. Some days were harder than others. He had to work with his doctor to find the right dosage. There were side effects initially decreased appetite, some trouble falling asleep that gradually improved.

But for the first time in months, Tyler didn't hate himself.

When he struggled to focus, he didn't spiral into self-loathing. He adjusted his approach. He took a movement break. He used a fidget. He asked for clarification on instructions instead of pretending he understood.

By the end of the semester, his grades had stabilized. He wasn't getting straight A's anymore he had mostly A's and B's, and one B-. And that was okay.

More importantly, his debate performance improved dramatically. He could remember his evidence. He could organize his thoughts mid-speech. He and Alex made it to the state finals.

He also had an honest conversation with his parents. They apologized for not believing him sooner. His dad admitted he'd been thinking of ADHD as an "excuse" rather than a real condition. His mom said she'd felt guilty like she'd failed him by not noticing sooner.

Tyler joined an online ADHD community and found hundreds of people who described experiences identical to his. He wasn't alone. He'd never been alone.

He started advocating for himself at school. When his AP Chem teacher made a dismissive comment about ADHD being "overdiagnosed," Tyler politely but firmly explained the neuroscience. Several classmates thanked him afterward.

One night in late January, Tyler sat at his desk finishing a history essay. It was 8:30 PM. He'd started at 6:00 PM, after dinner. Two and a half hours for a five-paragraph essay exactly the time it should take.

His medication had worn off by now, and he could feel the fog creeping back in. But he'd built systems that worked even without medication. He had an outline. He had a timer. He had a checklist.

He finished the essay, read through it once, and saved it.

His phone buzzed. Alex: *how's the essay going?*

Tyler: *just finished*

Alex: *show off*

Tyler smiled. A year ago, he would've been starting that essay at midnight, panicking, hating himself. Now he was done with time to spare.

He wasn't "cured." He still had ADHD. He always would. But he understood his brain now. He had tools. He had accommodations. He had people who believed him.

Junior year was still hard. But it was manageable. And that was enough.

Tyler looked at the college brochures stacked on his shelf. A year ago, college had seemed impossible just another place to fail. Now it seemed different. Challenging, yes. But possible.

He thought about Ms. Rodriguez, who had ADHD and was a successful teacher and coach. About the people in his online community with ADHD who were doctors, engineers, artists, parents, writers. About the understanding that ADHD wasn't a barrier to success it just meant he needed to build success differently.

Tyler closed his laptop and looked at his reflection in the dark window.

"I'm not lazy," he said out loud. "I'm not stupid. My brain works differently. And that's okay."

For the first time in his life, he actually believed it.

———

REFLECT

Tyler's story shows that ADHD doesn't always look like hyperactivity or obvious struggling. Sometimes the smartest, most capable students are the ones suffering in silence, using sheer willpower to compensate for executive function challenges until they can't anymore. If Tyler's experience resonates with you, you're not alone.

1. **Have you ever felt like Tyler succeeding on the outside while drowning on the inside?** What does that feel like for you?

   ____

   ____

   ____

   ____

2. **Tyler spent years thinking his struggles were about laziness or lack of intelligence. Have you blamed yourself for things that might actually be ADHD-related?** What would change if you reframed those struggles as neurological rather than personal failings?

   ____

   ____

   ____

---

3. **Tyler's parents initially didn't believe ADHD was real or relevant to him. Have you encountered skepticism about ADHD from parents, teachers, or even yourself?** How has that skepticism affected your willingness to seek support?

---

4. **The psychologist explained that Tyler had been "working ten times harder to get the same results" as his peers. Do you relate to this?** In what areas of your life do you feel like you're working exponentially harder than others for average outcomes?

---

5. **Tyler felt intense relief when he got his diagnosis finally having an explanation for his struggles. If you have (or had) a diagnosis, what emotions came with it?** If you're undiagnosed but suspect ADHD, what holds you back from seeking evaluation?

---

6. **Tyler's dad initially saw accommodations and medication as "excuses" rather than legitimate tools. How do you feel about using accommodations or medication?** What beliefs (yours or others') make it harder to accept the support you need?

____

____

____

____

7. **Tyler had to stop relying on willpower and memory and start using external systems (phone reminders, visual schedules, body doubling). What systems or tools have helped you?** What have you tried that didn't work?

____

____

____

____

8. **By the end, Tyler accepted that he might get B's instead of straight A's and that's okay. What would it look like for you to adjust your expectations to match your ADHD brain rather than constantly pushing yourself to meet neurotypical standards?**

____

____

____

____

ACT

This week, stop blaming yourself for ADHD struggles and start building external systems that work for your brain.

High intelligence can mask ADHD for years, but eventually demands exceed your ability to compensate through sheer brainpower. You're not lazy you're working harder than neurotypical peers just to achieve the same results. Your task is to stop relying on willpower alone and build external scaffolding.

Track your "invisible struggles" and build corresponding systems:

For three days, keep a simple log of moments when you struggle in ways others don't see. Write down:

- Reading the same paragraph 5+ times without retention → *Tomorrow: Try the "Pointer Method" (follow text with your finger or use a ruler to track lines while reading)*
- Spending 6 hours on 2 hours of homework → *Tomorrow: Use Pomodoro (25 min work, 5 min break) and see if focused bursts help*
- Forgetting test dates despite writing them down → *Tomorrow: Set 3 phone alarms per test 1 week before, 1 day before, morning of*
- Zoning out in class even when trying to focus → *Tomorrow: Take notes by hand, doodle while listening, or use fidget tools*

After three days, choose the ONE struggle that's costing you most (grades, time, stress). Build one external system to address it this week. Not five systems just one. Master it before adding more.

Then consider: If your struggles are invisible and exhausting, could medication or accommodations help? Many people with ADHD-Inattentive don't realize they qualify for support because their struggles aren't disruptive to others. Talk to a counselor or doctor about evaluation if you're working 3x harder than peers for the same results that's a sign you need more than willpower.

Important reminders:

- ADHD-Inattentive is "invisible" but equally valid and challenging as hyperactive presentations

- High intelligence masks ADHD until demands exceed your compensation abilities that's neurology, not laziness
- Working harder for the same results as peers means you need accommodations, not more effort
- Reading the same paragraph 5x isn't poor focus it's working memory deficit and needs external strategies
- External systems aren't "crutches" they're tools that do what your executive function can't
- Medication is legitimate treatment for a neurological condition, not weakness or cheating
- You're not failing you're trying to succeed in systems designed for different brains
- Academic accommodations are equity, not advantage they remove barriers you face that others don't

STORY 2: THE WAITING GAME

A STORY about learning that your brain operates on a different timeline and that's not the same as being behind.

Zara Martinez watched the clock tick from 11:47 to 11:48 AM. Seven minutes left in the math quiz. Around her, pencils scratched paper in a steady rhythm. Three students had already turned in their quizzes and were reading at their desks.

Zara was on problem four of fifteen.

Not because she didn't understand the material she did. She'd studied for hours. She knew how to solve these problems. But her brain needed time to process each step, to double-check, to make sure she wasn't making careless mistakes. And somehow, impossibly, that process ate up minutes like a hungry monster.

11:49.

She forced herself to move faster. Problem five. Read it. Read it again. What's it asking? Okay, set up the equation. Wait, did she read it right? Read it again. Yes. Okay, solve. Show your work. Check the answer. Does that make sense? Seems right. Move on.

11:50.

"Time's up," Ms. Chen announced. "Pencils down, please."

Zara had completed six problems.

As she handed in her quiz half-blank, half-finished Ms. Chen gave her a sympathetic look that made Zara's stomach twist. Not anger. Pity was worse.

This was her life. Always running out of time. Always behind. Always watching everyone else finish while she was still processing.

Zara had ADHD. She'd known since sixth grade, when her constant fidgeting, interrupting, and "not finishing anything you start" had finally led to an evaluation. The diagnosis explained some things why she blurted out answers, why she couldn't sit still, why she started a million projects and finished none.

But it didn't explain why everything took her so much longer than it took everyone else.

She wasn't stupid. Her teachers said she was "bright" and "capable." But capable students finished their work on time. Capable students didn't need extended time on every single test. Capable students didn't take an hour to write three paragraphs while their classmates cranked out full essays in forty minutes.

Her parents tried to be understanding. "You just need to manage your time better," her mom said, buying her a planner with color-coded sections. Zara used it for three days before forgetting it existed.

Her older brother Marcus, a junior, didn't help. "I don't get what takes you so long. Just do the work." He could finish homework in half the time Zara spent staring at the first problem.

Her best friend Lia was patient, but even she got frustrated sometimes. "Zara, come ON. We're going to miss the previews." They'd been trying to leave for the movies for twenty minutes while Zara looked for her phone, then her wallet, then remembered she needed to finish one assignment, then got distracted by a text.

Zara felt like she was living life on a five-second delay. Everyone else moved at normal speed while she buffered.

Freshman year was supposed to be a fresh start. New school, new people who didn't know her as "the spacey girl who's always late."

But within a month, the same patterns emerged.

She was late to first period four times in two weeks not because she woke up late, but because getting ready took forever. Brushing teeth somehow turned into fifteen minutes of staring in the mirror. Finding matching socks became an archaeological dig through her closet. By the time she was dressed and had her backpack, the bus was pulling away.

In English, she'd start writing an essay and discover she'd spent forty-five minutes on the introduction. Her mind would wander mid-sentence. She'd reread what she'd written, decide it was terrible, delete it, start over. Meanwhile, Lia would already be on her conclusion.

Group projects were the worst. She'd volunteer to do research and show up with half-done work while everyone else had finished their sections. They'd smile politely and redistribute her tasks. After the third time, they just stopped assigning her important parts.

"It's fine, Zara can make the poster," someone would say. Translation: Give her something that doesn't matter if she doesn't finish.

The worst part wasn't the academic struggle. It was the social judgment.

"You're so immature," a girl named Kelsey said in the locker room when Zara forgot her gym clothes for the third time.

"Why are you always so scattered?" another classmate asked when Zara showed up to a study group without her textbook.

"Are you even trying?" Marcus said when she asked him for help with an assignment due the next day that she'd had two weeks to complete.

Zara wanted to scream: *Yes, I'm trying! I'm trying so hard I'm exhausted! It's just that trying doesn't make my brain work faster!*

But she didn't say that. She just apologized. Again.

The breaking point came in late October.

Zara's biology teacher, Mr. Kumar, assigned a research project on genetics. Three weeks to complete. Choose a genetic disorder, research it, write a five-page paper, create a presentation. Due November 15th.

Zara wrote the date in her planner. She set phone reminders. She was NOT going to mess this up. This was 20% of her grade.

The first week, she researched. She found articles, read them (slowly, because she had to read everything twice to absorb it), took notes. Good. Progress.

The second week, she meant to start writing. But she couldn't figure out how to organize her notes. She tried three different outlines. None felt right. She asked Mr. Kumar for help. He explained the structure. She understood. But when she sat down to write, the blank page paralyzed her. She'd write a sentence, delete it, write another, delete it. By the end of week two, she had one paragraph.

Week three. Panic set in. She had four pages to write and a presentation to make. She could do this. She had to do this.

But her brain wouldn't cooperate. She'd sit down to work and suddenly remember she needed to text Lia back. Then she'd check Instagram. Then she'd remember she was supposed to be working and feel guilty. Then she'd start working, get three sentences in, and realize she needed to check if her source was credible. Down another research rabbit hole.

November 14th. The night before it was due. Zara had two pages written and no presentation.

She stayed up until 3 AM, crying and typing and hating herself. She finished three and a half pages not five and threw together a presentation with bullet points and no visuals.

She turned it in, exhausted and defeated.

Two weeks later, she got it back. C-.

Mr. Kumar's note: "Good ideas, but incomplete and rushed. You had three weeks. Time management is crucial."

Zara crumpled the paper and shoved it in her backpack.

Time management. Everyone said that like it was so simple. Like she just needed to try harder, plan better, be more organized.

But she HAD tried. She'd done everything right written it down, set reminders, started early. And she'd still failed. Because no matter how much time she had, it was never enough.

That afternoon, Zara sat in the counseling office, crying harder than she'd cried in years.

Mrs. Patterson, the school counselor, handed her tissues and waited patiently for Zara to calm down.

"I can't do this," Zara said. "Everyone keeps saying I need to manage my time better, but I don't know how. I try so hard and it's never enough. I'm never fast enough."

"Tell me what happened with the biology project," Mrs. Patterson said gently.

Zara explained the three weeks, the good intentions, the constant feeling of running out of time, the all-nighter, the C-.

Mrs. Patterson nodded. "Do you know what ADHD time blindness is?"

Zara shook her head.

"It's when your brain doesn't perceive time passing the way neurotypical brains do. Three weeks might feel like plenty of time intellectually, but your ADHD brain doesn't translate that into actionable steps. And then there's processing speed some people with ADHD take longer to complete tasks not because they don't understand, but because their brains need more time to process information."

"So I'm just... slow?"

"No. You're operating on a different timeline. That's not the same as being slow or unintelligent. It means your brain needs different supports." She paused. "Have you heard the phrase 'ADHD tax?'"

"No."

"It's the extra time, money, and energy that people with ADHD spend just to function at a baseline that comes naturally to neurotypical people. You're not bad at time management because you're not trying you're working with a brain that experiences time fundamentally differently."

Something in Zara's chest loosened. "So it's not just me being immature or lazy?"

"Not even a little bit. And there are strategies we can implement. But first, you need to understand: the timeline that works for your peers might not work for you. And that's okay. We need to find YOUR timeline."

Over the next month, Mrs. Patterson worked with Zara to build what she called "ADHD-friendly systems."

Step one: External time tracking. Zara couldn't rely on her internal sense of time, so she needed external cues. Mrs. Patterson helped her set up:

- Visual timers on her desk at home (seeing time pass helped her brain register it)
- Phone alarms for task transitions
- Time-blocking in her calendar with specific tasks assigned to specific hours

Step two: Breaking projects into micro-deadlines. Instead of "research paper due in three weeks," Zara worked with Mrs. Patterson to create mini-deadlines:

- Day 1-3: Research and take notes
- Day 4: Create outline
- Day 5-7: Write introduction and first body paragraph
- Day 8-10: Second and third body paragraphs
- And so on...

Each small deadline felt manageable. Each one had a specific task, not just "work on project."

Step three: Time cushions. Neurotypical students might need thirty minutes to write an essay introduction. Zara needed an hour. That wasn't failure that was her brain's processing speed. Mrs. Patterson helped her plan accordingly: estimate how long neurotypical students would take, then multiply by two for Zara's timeline.

Step four: Accommodations. Mrs. Patterson helped Zara formalize a 504 plan that included:

- Extended time on all tests and quizzes (time-and-a-half)
- Extended deadlines on projects (discussed with teachers in advance)
- Permission to use timers and headphones
- Access to project planning templates

Zara was hesitant about the accommodations. "Won't teachers think I'm getting special treatment?"

"You're getting equitable treatment," Mrs. Patterson corrected. "The goal isn't to give you an advantage it's to remove the disadvantage your ADHD creates. If a student needed glasses to see the board, we wouldn't call that special treatment. This is the same."

Step five: Reframing the narrative. This was the hardest part. Zara had spent years internalizing the message that she was immature, lazy, scattered, irresponsible. Mrs. Patterson helped her rewrite that story:

- "I'm always behind" became "I operate on a different timeline"

- "I can't manage time" became "My brain experiences time differently, so I need different tools"
- "Everyone else is faster" became "Everyone's brain works differently mine needs more processing time, and that's okay"

The first test of these new systems came in December with a history project.

Mr. Washington assigned a research paper on the Civil Rights Movement. Two weeks to complete. Five pages minimum.

Old Zara would have panicked. New Zara well, she still panicked a little but she also had a plan.

She sat down with Mrs. Patterson and broke the project into micro-deadlines:

- Days 1-2: Research (3 sources minimum)
- Day 3: Outline
- Days 4-5: Introduction + first body paragraph
- Days 6-7: Second body paragraph
- Days 8-9: Third body paragraph
- Days 10-11: Conclusion + works cited
- Days 12-13: Editing and final review
- Day 14: Submit

She put each deadline in her phone calendar with alerts. She set visual timers for work sessions forty-five minutes of work, fifteen-minute break. She gave herself extra time for each task, building in cushions for the inevitable distractions.

And when she sat down to work on Day 1, she didn't judge herself for taking three hours to read articles that her classmates probably read in forty-five minutes. She was on HER timeline. That was okay.

Day 4, when she spent two hours writing just the introduction, she didn't spiral into self-hatred. She was processing. Her brain needed time. She adjusted her schedule slightly and kept going.

By Day 10, she'd written four pages. She told Mr. Washington she needed one extra day for editing. He agreed her 504 plan allowed for reasonable deadline extensions with advance notice.

On Day 15, she submitted a five-page paper she was actually proud of.

Two weeks later, she got it back.

B+.

Mr. Washington's note: "Excellent research and thoughtful analysis. Well done, Zara."

She stared at the paper, tears blurring the words. Not tears of frustration this time. Relief. Pride. Maybe even a little bit of joy.

She'd done it. Not on anyone else's timeline. On hers.

Things didn't magically become easy. Zara still struggled. She still needed extended time. She still took longer than her peers to complete tasks.

But she stopped seeing that as a moral failing.

When Marcus complained about her taking too long to get ready, she said calmly, "My brain needs more transition time. I'm working on it, but I need you to stop making me feel bad about it."

When a teacher questioned her extended-time accommodation, saying, "Don't you think that's unfair to other students?" she replied, "Would you say glasses are unfair to students with perfect vision? Accommodations aren't advantages. They're equity."

When Lia got impatient waiting for her to finish getting ready for the movies, Zara texted ahead: "I need 20 extra minutes. I know that's annoying, but my brain just works slower. I'm sorry."

Lia texted back: "It's not annoying. I'll wait."

Freshman year ended. Zara's grades weren't perfect she had mostly B's, a couple of C's, one A in art. But they were honest grades that reflected her actual learning, not her inability to finish tests in the allotted time.

More importantly, she'd stopped hating herself.

On the last day of school, Zara met with Mrs. Patterson for their final check-in.

"How are you feeling about next year?" Mrs. Patterson asked.

"Nervous," Zara admitted. "But... better. I know what I need now. I know I'm not broken."

"You were never broken. You just needed different tools."

Zara smiled. "Can I ask you something? Do you think I'll ever be as fast as everyone else?"

Mrs. Patterson considered this carefully. "Maybe not. Some people's brains just process more slowly that's neurology, not effort. But here's the thing: speed isn't the same as capability. You can produce excellent work. It might take you longer, and that's okay. The goal isn't to become neurotypical. It's to build a life that works for YOUR brain."

Zara nodded. For the first time, she actually believed that was possible.

That summer, she didn't magically get faster. She still needed more time to get ready. She still took twice as long as Marcus to complete chores. She still processed information at her own pace.

But she stopped apologizing for it.

When she started sophomore year, she advocated for herself from day one. She met with each teacher, explained her 504 plan, and calmly requested the accommodations she needed. She used timers. She built in time cushions. She broke big projects into micro-deadlines.

And when classmates complained about homework taking forever, Zara thought: *Welcome to my world. Except I've learned how to survive it.*

One afternoon in October, Zara's biology teacher announced a three-week research project. Around her, students groaned.

Zara pulled out her planner and started breaking the project into micro-deadlines. Day 1: Research. Day 2: More research. Day 3: Outline...

The girl next to her leaned over. "What are you doing?"

"Planning," Zara said. "I have ADHD, so I need to break big projects into smaller pieces or I'll end up doing everything the night before."

"Oh my god, can you teach me how to do that? I always end up pulling all-nighters."

Zara smiled. "Sure."

By the end of class, she'd helped three students create micro-dead-line schedules for the project.

Turned out, Zara's "different timeline" strategies didn't just work for ADHD brains. They worked for anyone who struggled with long-term planning.

Maybe her brain wasn't behind. Maybe it was just different. And maybe different had value.

She thought about freshman-year Zara, crying in Mrs. Patterson's office, convinced she was broken.

If she could talk to that girl now, she'd say: *You're not behind. You're not slow. You're not immature. Your brain operates on a different time-line, and that's not a flaw it's just how you're wired. Stop trying to fit into someone else's timeline. Build your own.*

Zara closed her planner and smiled.

For the first time in her life, she wasn't racing to catch up to everyone else.

She was running her own race, at her own pace.

And she was winning.

––––––

REFLECT

Zara's story illustrates one of the most frustrating aspects of ADHD: time blindness and different processing speeds. If you've ever felt like you're constantly behind, always running out of time, or taking twice as long as everyone else to complete tasks, you're not alone and you're not broken.

1. **Zara described feeling like she was "living life on a five-second delay" while everyone else moved at normal speed. Do you relate to this feeling?** In what situations do you feel like you're buffering while everyone else has already loaded?

____
____
____

____

2. **People kept telling Zara to "manage your time better," but the problem wasn't effort it was that her brain experienced time differently. Have you been given advice that doesn't address the actual neurological challenge you're facing?** What would be more helpful than "just try harder"?

____
____
____

____

3. **Zara felt judged as "immature," "scattered," and "irresponsible" because tasks took her longer. What labels have been applied to you because of your ADHD processing speed or time blindness?** How have those labels affected your self-perception?

____
____
____

____

4. **The counselor explained that Zara was "operating on a different timeline" rather than being "behind." How does that reframe resonate with you?** What changes if you stop measuring yourself against neurotypical timelines?

____
____
____

____

5. **Zara had to multiply time estimates by two to account for her processing speed what neurotypical students could do in 30 minutes took her an hour. Do you have a sense of how much extra time YOUR brain needs compared to standard estimates?** How could you start building that into your planning?

____
____
____
____

6. **Extended time accommodations made Zara feel like she was getting "special treatment" rather than equity. How do you feel about asking for accommodations?** What beliefs (yours or others') make it harder to accept the support you need?

____
____
____
____

7. **Zara struggled with long-term projects because three weeks felt both like "plenty of time" and "somehow not enough." Do you experience time blindness with long-term assignments?** What does that look like for you?

____
____
____
____

8. **By the end, Zara stopped apologizing for needing more time and started advocating for herself. What would it look like for you to stop apologizing for your brain's timeline and start building systems that actually work for you?**

____

____

____

____

ACT

This week, accept that you operate on a different timeline than neurotypical people and build your schedule around that reality.

ADHD time blindness and processing speed differences mean everything takes you longer not because you're slow or behind, but because your brain operates on a different timeline. You're not late; you're on ADHD time. Your task is to stop trying to match neurotypical speed and start planning for your actual processing needs.

Calculate your personal "time multiplier" and rebuild your schedule:

For three days, track how long tasks actually take you versus how long they "should" take:

- Getting ready in the morning: Neurotypical estimate = 30 min, Your reality = ______ min
- Essay writing: Neurotypical estimate = 2 hours, Your reality = ______ min
- Quiz completion: Neurotypical estimate = 20 min, Your reality = ______ min
- Project work session: Neurotypical estimate = 1 hour, Your reality = ______ min

After three days, calculate your average multiplier. If tasks consistently take you 2x as long, your time multiplier is 2x. If they take 1.5x as long, that's your multiplier.

Now apply this to one major upcoming task:

- Teacher says: "This project should take 3 hours"
- Your calculation: 3 hours × your multiplier = your realistic time needed
- Your action: Block that FULL amount of time in your schedule, not the neurotypical estimate

Also, request extended time accommodations if you don't have them. Processing speed differences are a documented ADHD challenge covered by disability law. Extended time isn't giving you an advantage it's giving you the time your brain actually needs to process and demonstrate your knowledge.

Important reminders:

- You're not "behind" you operate on a different timeline, and that's neurological, not personal failing
- Time multipliers are real if tasks consistently take you 2x longer, that's your brain's processing speed, not laziness
- "Neurotypical time estimates" don't apply to you use your actual time data instead
- Extended time accommodations are legitimate medical support, not special treatment
- Micro-deadlines (daily mini-goals) work better than distant final deadlines for ADHD time blindness
- Time cushions prevent the panic of running out of time always add buffer time
- Stop apologizing for needing more time you're working with different processing architecture
- Different timeline doesn't mean inadequate it means different, and different requires different planning

CHAPTER 3

STORY 3: THE HYPERFOCUS TRAP

A STORY about learning that your superpower can also be your kryptonite and how to use it without letting it use you.

Mason Rivera's fingers flew across the keyboard, lines of code streaming down his screen in a waterfall of logic and syntax. His game was almost done just needed to debug this one function and implement the final boss battle mechanics. He could see it so clearly in his mind: the player dodging attacks, the health bar decreasing, the victory screen with the credits he'd designed...

"Mason! Dinner!"

His mom's voice was background noise. Not now. He was so close. Just a few more lines. Just needed to test this collision detection algorithm. If he stopped now, he'd lose his train of thought, lose the elegant solution he'd been building for the past

He glanced at the clock. 7:30 PM.

Wait. That couldn't be right.

He'd sat down to code at 2:00 PM. After lunch. Except... he'd never eaten lunch, had he?

Mason's stomach growled, suddenly making itself known. His back ached. When had he last moved? His water bottle sat empty beside him. His phone showed six missed texts.

"MASON! Dinner's getting cold!"

"Coming!" he called, saving his work. He stood up too fast and his vision swam. His legs had fallen asleep.

This happened more often than he wanted to admit.

Mason had ADHD. The combined type both inattentive and hyperactive, though the hyperactivity mostly showed up as a restless mind rather than a restless body. He'd been diagnosed at ten, after years of teachers complaining he "wasn't reaching his potential."

The thing about ADHD that confused everyone including Mason was the hyperfocus.

"If you have attention deficit disorder, how can you focus on video games for eight hours straight?" his dad would ask, frustrated when Mason couldn't focus on homework for twenty minutes.

The answer: ADHD wasn't a deficit of attention. It was a dysregulation of attention. Mason couldn't choose what he focused on his brain did. And when his brain decided something was interesting, it was like falling into a black hole. Time disappeared. The world disappeared. Nothing existed except the code, the problem, the flow state.

It was the closest thing to magic Mason had ever experienced.

It was also ruining his life.

Senior year was supposed to be Mason's year. He'd survived three years of high school, maintained decent grades (mostly B's and A's in classes he liked, C's in classes he didn't), and made it to the finish line. College applications were due in two months. He just had to keep it together a little longer.

But "keeping it together" was getting harder.

Mason's passion was game development. He'd been coding since he was twelve, teaching himself Python, then C++, then Unity. He'd built a portfolio of small games nothing commercial, but impressive for a seventeen-year-old. He spent every free moment designing mechanics, writing code, creating pixel art.

The problem was that "every free moment" had started bleeding into moments that weren't supposed to be free.

Like last week, when he'd been working on his college essay. He'd opened his laptop, stared at the blank document for ten minutes, felt his brain sliding away in boredom. Then he'd thought, *I'll just check my game project real quick. Five minutes.*

Four hours later, he'd implemented a new enemy AI and hadn't written a single word of his essay.

Or two weeks ago, when his best friend Jordan had asked him to come over after school. Mason had said yes, but then he'd started fixing a bug in his code and suddenly it was 9 PM and he'd completely forgotten. Jordan had texted: *Are you coming or what?* Mason had apologized, but Jordan had been irritated. It wasn't the first time.

Or yesterday, when he'd skipped lunch to work on his game in the library, then skipped dinner too, and realized at 11 PM that he'd eaten nothing but a granola bar all day.

His mom was worried. "You're obsessed with that computer. It's not healthy."

"I'm not obsessed. I'm passionate."

"Passion shouldn't make you forget to eat or sleep or see your friends."

But that was the thing about hyperfocus. When Mason was in it, he didn't feel hungry. Didn't feel tired. Didn't notice time passing. It was like his brain had an ON switch and an OFF switch, with nothing in between. Either he couldn't focus at all, or he couldn't stop focusing.

All or nothing. That was ADHD in a nutshell.

The real problem started in October.

Mason's AP Lit teacher, Ms. Washington, assigned a research paper on *Hamlet*. Ten pages. Due November 10th. Worth 30% of their grade.

Mason wrote the due date in his planner. He knew it was important. He knew he needed to start early.

But every time he tried to work on it, his brain revolted. Shakespeare was boring. Literary analysis was torture. He'd stare at the assignment prompt, feel his motivation drain away like water through a sieve, and then almost without conscious decision he'd open his game project instead.

Just for a few minutes. Just to clear my head.

And then it was three hours later and he hadn't written anything.

This happened day after day. Week after week. Meanwhile, his game was getting better and better. He'd implemented a save system, improved the graphics, added a soundtrack he'd composed himself. He was so proud of it.

But the paper wasn't getting written.

November 9th. The night before the paper was due. Mason had written exactly zero pages.

He stayed up all night, mainlining coffee and panic, forcing himself to write even though his brain was screaming at him that this was the most boring task in human history. He couldn't get into flow. Couldn't hyperfocus. Because his brain only hyperfocused on things that interested it, and Shakespeare's use of symbolism definitely wasn't on that list.

By 6 AM, he'd written seven pages of rambling, barely-coherent analysis.

He turned it in exhausted and defeated.

Two weeks later, he got it back. D+.

Ms. Washington's note: "This feels rushed and incomplete. I know you're capable of better work. See me after class."

After class, Ms. Washington asked gently, "What happened, Mason? This isn't like you."

"I just... couldn't focus on it."

"But your game design project for Computer Science was excellent. Mr. Park showed it to me. You put incredible effort into that."

"That's different. That's interesting."

"So you can focus just not on things you find boring?"

Mason felt defensive. "I have ADHD. I can't help what my brain focuses on."

Ms. Washington nodded thoughtfully. "I believe you. But here's what concerns me: you're about to graduate. College will have required classes you find boring. Jobs will have tasks you don't want to do. Your hyperfocus is an incredible gift but only if you learn to manage it. Right now, it's managing you."

Her words stung because they were true.

That night, Mason's parents sat him down for a conversation.

"We need to talk about the computer," his dad said.

Mason's stomach dropped. "What about it?"

"You're on it too much. Your grades are slipping. You're not socializing. You're not taking care of yourself."

"I'm working on my game. It's not just playing I'm learning skills."

"We know," his mom said. "And we're proud of your talent. But it's becoming unhealthy. You're disappearing into that screen for entire days."

"So what do you want me to do? Quit? This is what I'm good at!"

"We want you to have balance," his dad said. "We're thinking of setting screen time limits."

"I'm seventeen! You can't just "

"We can, actually," his mom said firmly. "Because what you're doing isn't sustainable. You forget to eat. You stay up all night. You're missing homework assignments. Something has to change."

Mason stormed upstairs, furious. They didn't understand. When he was coding, he felt competent. Powerful. Like he could build entire worlds with his mind. The rest of school felt meaningless in comparison.

But lying in bed that night, he admitted something uncomfortable: they were right.

He was disappearing into hyperfocus. And while it felt amazing in the moment, the aftermath was always the same neglected friendships, missed obligations, crashed energy, guilt and shame.

His superpower was becoming his kryptonite.

The next day, Mason made an appointment with his school counselor, Mr. Chen.

"Tell me what's going on," Mr. Chen said.

Mason explained everything the hyperfocus on coding, the inability to focus on schoolwork, the all-or-nothing attention, the way he lost hours without realizing it, the mounting college app stress, the concerned parents.

Mr. Chen listened, then asked, "Do you know what hyperfocus is in the context of ADHD?"

"Yeah, it's like... intense concentration on something interesting."

"It's more specific than that. Hyperfocus is a state of intense, sustained attention on a single task that activates the ADHD brain's reward system. It happens because ADHD brains are chronically under-stimulated they're seeking that dopamine hit. Coding gives you that. Shakespeare doesn't."

"So how do I make myself focus on boring stuff?"

"That's the wrong question. The better question is: how do you harness your hyperfocus productively while also meeting your other obligations?"

Mr. Chen explained several strategies:

1. Schedule hyperfocus time intentionally. Instead of letting it happen randomly, block out specific times for passion projects. "Saturday 2-6 PM: Game development." Then when hyperfocus tries to pull you in at other times, you can tell yourself: I'll get to do this on Saturday.

2. Use timers to break hyperfocus. Set an alarm before starting. When it goes off, stop even if you're not ready. This trains your brain that hyperfocus has boundaries.

3. Front-load obligations before allowing hyperfocus. Make a rule: no game development until homework is done. Use hyperfocus as a reward, not an escape.

4. Build in hyperfocus breaks. ADHD brains need interesting stimulation to function. Instead of fighting that, work with it. Thirty minutes of boring homework, then ten minutes of coding. Repeat.

5. Use hyperfocus interests to tackle boring tasks. Could Mason gamify his homework? Turn his paper into a coding challenge? Find any connection between his passion and his obligations?

6. Address the crash. Hyperfocus depletes mental energy and ignores physical needs. Build in post-hyperfocus recovery: eat, hydrate, move your body, sleep.

"The goal isn't to eliminate hyperfocus," Mr. Chen said. "It's to become the driver instead of the passenger."

Mason started implementing the strategies, though it was harder than he'd expected.

Week 1: Timer experiments

He set a two-hour timer before starting to code. When it went off, he forced himself to stop, even though his brain screamed at him to keep going. The first few times, it felt like tearing himself away from something vital. But gradually, it got easier. His brain started learning: *I can come back to this later.*

Week 2: Front-loading obligations

He made a strict rule: homework before game development. No exceptions. This meant some days he didn't get to code at all because homework took longer than expected. That was frustrating. But his grades started improving.

Week 3: Scheduled hyperfocus windows

Every Saturday and Sunday, 1-5 PM was his designated coding time. Four hours of guilt-free hyperfocus. Knowing he had this time helped him resist the urge to code during the week. When his brain tried to pull him toward his game project on a Tuesday night, he could say: *I'll have time on Saturday. Right now, I need to focus on this.*

Week 4: Physical needs checklist

He set alarms every two hours: "Have you eaten? Had water? Stood up?" during coding sessions. It felt annoying at first, but he realized he'd been regularly going six, seven, eight hours without food or water. No wonder he kept crashing afterward.

The strategies helped. But they also highlighted something uncomfortable: managing ADHD took constant effort. Neurotypical people didn't have to set alarms to remember to eat. They didn't have to schedule their own interests like doctor's appointments. They didn't have to fight their own brain's pull toward what it found rewarding.

It was exhausting.

But it was working.

The turning point came in mid-November, at a college fair.

Mason visited the booth for a game design program he'd been interested in. The admission counselor asked about his portfolio.

"I've been developing games for five years," Mason said. "Mostly indie projects, nothing commercial, but I've learned Unity, C++, pixel art, sound design..."

"Do you have examples?"

Mason pulled up his portfolio on his phone. The counselor's eyes widened. "This is impressive. Especially for high school. What's your process?"

"I, uh... I hyperfocus. I have ADHD, and when I get into a project, I can work on it for hours without stopping. It's kind of my superpower."

"Hyperfocus is definitely a superpower in game development," the counselor said. "The best developers I know are people who can lose themselves in problem-solving for days at a time. The industry actually has a lot of ADHD folks not diagnosed, maybe, but the pattern's there."

Something clicked in Mason's brain. His hyperfocus wasn't just a liability. It was an actual, legitimate strength in his chosen field.

"The trick," the counselor continued, "is learning to balance it. Game development has crunch times where hyperfocus is great. But you also need to eat, sleep, maintain relationships. Burnout is real in this industry. So if you can learn now, in high school, how to harness hyperfocus without letting it destroy your health you'll be ahead of most people in the field."

Mason left the college fair feeling something he hadn't felt in months: hopeful.

His ADHD hyperfocus wasn't something to fix or eliminate. It was something to understand and channel.

Over the next month, Mason refined his approach.

He started treating his game development as legitimate work not a distraction, but a skill he was cultivating. He included his projects on his college applications, wrote his personal essay about learning to harness hyperfocus, and submitted his portfolio as a supplemental material.

He also rebuilt his boundaries:

Daily structure:

- School days: No coding until homework complete
- Weekend mornings: Chores, family time, social obligations
- Weekend afternoons: 4-hour hyperfocus blocks for game dev
- Evenings: Flexible, but with timers and breaks

Physical needs protocol:

- Set phone alarm every 90 minutes during coding
- When alarm goes off: stand, stretch, eat/drink something, check in with body
- Maximum coding session: 4 hours, then mandatory 30-minute break

Social maintenance:

- One non-negotiable friend hangout per week (even if brain wants to code)
- Respond to texts within 24 hours (set reminder if necessary)
- Tell friends in advance if he'd be less available: "I'm deep in a project this weekend, but let's hang Monday"

Project boundaries:

- Every project has a scope document and timeline
- When hitting timeline, stop even if not "perfect"
- Practice finishing things, not just starting them

It wasn't perfect. Mason still sometimes lost track of time. Still sometimes chose coding over sleep. Still sometimes struggled to focus on boring schoolwork.

But he was getting better.

And his game? He finished it. Actually finished it. Not "perfect," not "exactly as envisioned," but done. Complete. Playable.

He submitted it to a student game design competition and won an honorable mention.

In January, Mason got his first college acceptance letter. The game design program he'd applied to. Full scholarship.

The acceptance letter specifically mentioned his portfolio: "Your demonstrated passion and skill in game development, combined with your thoughtful essay about learning to harness hyperfocus, shows maturity and self-awareness that will serve you well in our rigorous program."

His parents cried. Mason stared at the letter, almost unable to believe it.

His "obsession" had gotten him into college. His "problem" had become his greatest asset.

That night, Jordan came over to celebrate. They'd rebuilt their friendship over the past few months. Mason had apologized for all the missed hangouts, explained what he'd been learning about hyperfocus, and made a conscious effort to be more present.

"I'm proud of you, man," Jordan said. "You figured your stuff out."

"I'm still figuring it out," Mason admitted. "I'll probably always be figuring it out. But at least now I understand what's happening."

"So are you going to become a famous game developer and forget all of us?"

Mason laughed. "No. I'm going to become a famous game developer who remembers to eat lunch and text his friends back."

Senior year ended. Mason graduated with a 3.4 GPA not perfect, but respectable. More importantly, he graduated with self-knowledge that most people didn't have at seventeen.

He understood his brain. He knew his strengths and his vulnerabilities. He had strategies for managing both.

The week before leaving for college, Mason did one final deep coding session a new game idea he wanted to prototype before school started. But this time, he set a timer. He ate lunch. He took breaks. He stopped at 6 PM, even though he wanted to keep going.

And when he closed his laptop, instead of feeling guilty or crashed or depleted, he felt satisfied.

He'd used his hyperfocus. It hadn't used him.

Mason looked at the acceptance letter on his wall, next to his computer. His mom had framed it.

"Your demonstrated passion and skill... combined with your thoughtful essay about learning to harness hyperfocus..."

He'd spent so many years thinking his ADHD was just a collection of problems: Can't focus. Can't sit still. Can't stop focusing. Can't start boring tasks.

But hyperfocus wasn't a problem. It was a different way of engaging with the world. A way that came with challenges, yes but also with gifts.

The trick was learning to drive instead of being driven.

Mason opened a new document and started outlining his next game. But this time, he set a timer first.

Two hours. Then dinner with his family. Then maybe a movie with Jordan.

Balance. That was the goal. Not perfection. Just balance.

And for the first time in his life, Mason felt like he might actually achieve it.

————

REFLECT

Mason's story captures the paradox of ADHD hyperfocus: it's simultaneously your greatest strength and your biggest vulnerability. When you can disappear into a project for hours, losing track of time and the world around you, it feels like a superpower until you realize you've neglected everything else that matters.

1. **Mason described hyperfocus as "the closest thing to magic" but also something that was "ruining his life." Do you experience this paradox?** What activities trigger hyperfocus for you, and how has it both helped and hurt you?

____

____

____

____

2. **When Mason's dad asked, "If you have attention deficit disorder, how can you focus on video games for eight hours straight?" he touched on a common misunderstanding about ADHD. How do you explain the difference between not being able to focus on boring tasks versus hyperfocusing on interesting ones?** Have people used your ability to hyperfocus as "proof" that you don't really have ADHD?

____

____

____

____

3. **Mason regularly forgot to eat, drink water, sleep, and respond to friends when hyperfocused. What basic needs or responsibilities do you neglect during hyperfocus?** What's the typical "crash" like afterward?

____

____

____

____

4. **The counselor said Mason was "the passenger, not the driver" of his hyperfocus. Do you relate to this feeling of hyperfocus controlling you rather than you controlling it?** What does it feel like when you try to stop hyperfocusing before you're "ready"?

____

____

____

____

5. **Mason could spend twelve hours coding but couldn't write a five-paragraph essay. His brain only hyperfocused on things that interested it. How does this all-or-nothing attention pattern show up in your academic or work life?** What tasks can you hyperfocus on versus tasks where you can't focus at all?

____

____

____

____

6. **Mason's hyperfocus became his career asset game development actually values people who can "lose themselves in problem-solving for days." Have you identified careers, hobbies, or skills where your hyperfocus is genuinely an advantage?** How might you build a life around your hyperfocus strengths rather than constantly fighting them?

____

____

____

____

7. **The strategies Mason learned involved setting timers, scheduling hyperfocus windows, and front-loading obligations. What attempts have you made to manage hyperfocus?** What's worked and what hasn't?

____

____

____

____

8. **Mason had to practice "finishing things, not just starting them" and stopping projects even when they weren't "perfect." Do you struggle with completion because hyperfocus makes you want to keep perfecting and improving?** How does perfectionism intersect with your hyperfocus?

____

____

____

____

ACT

This week, schedule your hyperfocus intentionally instead of letting it control you.

ADHD hyperfocus is both gift and curse you can produce exceptional work through sustained concentration, but you can also disappear into projects at the wrong times, neglect basic needs, and damage relationships. Your task is to harness hyperfocus as a tool you control rather than an impulse that controls you.

Create "Hyperfocus Windows" in your schedule:

Identify one passion project or interest area where you tend to hyperfocus (gaming, coding, art, research, building something, writing, etc.). Instead of trying to stop hyperfocusing or feeling guilty about it, schedule it intentionally:

This week, create one 3-4 hour "Hyperfocus Window":

- Choose a day and time: "Saturday 2pm-6pm is my hyperfocus window"
- Front-load obligations FIRST: Finish homework, chores, and responsibilities BEFORE the window opens
- Set up your environment: Food/water/snacks prepared, bathroom break taken, phone charged
- Set a timer to END the hyperfocus window: Use multiple loud alarms ADHD brains are notorious for ignoring timers
- Build in a physical transition: When timer goes off, immediately stand up, stretch, walk outside for 5 minutes before returning to other tasks

The key insight: Scheduled hyperfocus is productive. Unscheduled hyperfocus is escape. When you give yourself permission to hyperfocus at designated times, the urge to hyperfocus at wrong times often decreases because your brain knows it'll get that dopamine reward later.

Also this week: Notice if you're using hyperfocus to avoid difficult tasks. If you hyperfocus on a game when you have a test tomorrow, that's avoidance, not productivity. The scheduled window only happens AFTER obligations are done.

Important reminders:

- Hyperfocus is an ADHD trait with both benefits (exceptional work) and costs (neglected needs, tunnel vision)
- Scheduling hyperfocus isn't indulgent it's strategic management of a powerful cognitive state
- Front-loading obligations prevents hyperfocus from becoming avoidance or escape
- Timers are essential but ADHD brains need MULTIPLE alarms to actually stop hyperfocusing
- Physical needs during hyperfocus (food, water, bathroom, movement) must be planned in advance
- Hyperfocus on passions can lead to expertise, careers, and exceptional achievement when managed well
- Unmanaged hyperfocus damages relationships people feel ignored when you disappear for hours
- The goal isn't to eliminate hyperfocus it's to channel it productively and protect what else matters

CHAPTER 4
STORY 4: THE EXPLOSION POINT

A STORY about learning that emotional intensity isn't the same as being "too sensitive" and that your feelings are valid even when they're overwhelming.

Jasmine Thompson stared at the test paper on her desk, her vision blurring with tears she refused to let fall. B+. Ninety-two percent. Objectively good. She knew that. Logically, she understood that a B+ was a perfectly respectable grade.

But her chest felt like it was caving in. Her throat tightened. The disappointment crashed over her like a tsunami, drowning out every rational thought.

She'd studied for hours. She'd done everything right. And it still wasn't enough. She'd never be enough.

"Nice work, Jasmine," her teacher said, moving past her desk.

Jasmine managed a smile that felt like cracking glass. The second Ms. Rivera turned away, Jasmine crumpled the paper and shoved it into her backpack, blinking hard against the burning in her eyes.

It was just a grade. Why did it feel like the end of the world?

Jasmine had ADHD. Combined type, diagnosed in seventh grade after years of teachers saying she was "too emotional" and "too reactive." The diagnosis explained some things the fidgeting, the spacing out, the inability to start homework until the night before it was due.

But it didn't explain why her emotions felt like explosions.

A friend canceling plans didn't just disappoint her it devastated her, convinced her that nobody actually liked her, sent her spiraling into anxiety for hours.

A critical comment from a teacher didn't just sting it felt like a personal attack, a confirmation that she was stupid and would never succeed.

A text left on "read" didn't just annoy her it triggered panic that she'd said something wrong, that the friendship was over, that everyone was talking about her.

Her emotions went from zero to one hundred in seconds. No middle ground. No gradual escalation. Just calm one moment, then suddenly drowning in feeling the next.

And the worst part? Everyone told her she was overreacting.

"It's not that serious, Jasmine."

"You're being too sensitive."

"You need to calm down."

"Why are you crying over something so small?"

She'd heard it so many times she'd started to believe it. Maybe she was too sensitive. Maybe she was just dramatic. Maybe something was fundamentally broken inside her that made her feel everything too much.

Tenth grade started rough and got rougher.

In September, Jasmine's best friend Maya mentioned offhandedly that she was hanging out with their mutual friend Emma that weekend. "Just the two of us. We're going thrifting."

Jasmine smiled and said, "Cool, have fun."

But inside, something shattered.

Why didn't they invite me? Do they not want me there? Are they talking about me? Are they tired of me? Am I too much? I knew it. Everyone eventually realizes I'm too much.

By that evening, Jasmine had spiraled completely. She lay on her bed, crying, convinced her friends secretly hated her. When Maya texted her a funny meme, Jasmine couldn't even respond. The gap between her rational brain (they're just hanging out, it's fine) and her emotional brain (you're being excluded, they don't want you) was unbridgeable.

Her mom knocked on her door. "Dinner's ready."

"I'm not hungry."

"Jasmine, you need to eat."

"I said I'm not hungry!" The words came out sharper than she meant. Anger flared suddenly, hot and overwhelming. Why couldn't her mom just leave her alone?

Her mom's voice turned firm. "Don't use that tone with me."

And just like that, Jasmine was crying again. Not anger anymore now it was guilt and shame. "I'm sorry," she sobbed. "I'm sorry. I don't know why I'm like this."

Her mom softened, sitting on the edge of the bed. "Honey, what's going on?"

"Nothing. Everything. I don't know." How could she explain that

Maya's innocent comment about weekend plans had triggered a complete emotional meltdown? It sounded ridiculous even to her.

October brought more explosions.

In English class, Mr. Torres handed back essays. Jasmine got an A-, with a note: "Good analysis, but watch your comma usage."

A reasonable, constructive comment. Jasmine knew that intellectually.

But reading it felt like being punched. Her face burned. Her eyes stung. The shame was instant and total. She couldn't focus for the rest of class, too busy mentally spiraling: *I can't even use commas correctly. I'm never going to be a good writer. Why do I even try?*

At lunch, Emma was talking about her weekend plans. "My mom's taking me to this concert. It's going to be amazing."

"That sounds fun," Jasmine said, trying to sound normal.

"Yeah, I'm so excited. I've been waiting for this for months."

Something in Jasmine's chest twisted. Not jealousy, exactly. More like... intense longing? Sadness? She couldn't even name it. But suddenly she felt like crying again.

What is wrong with me? Why am I about to cry because my friend is going to a concert?

She excused herself to the bathroom and locked herself in a stall, breathing hard, trying to get control. The emotions were too big. Too fast. Too much.

She was so tired of feeling everything so intensely.

The real breaking point came in late October.

Jasmine had been working on a group project with three classmates. She'd done her part more than her part, actually. She'd stayed up late organizing their presentation, making it look professional, making sure everyone's sections flowed together.

The day before they were supposed to present, one group member, Derek, texted the group chat: "Hey, I rewrote Jasmine's intro. It was kind of confusing. No offense."

Jasmine stared at her phone.

Her intro hadn't been confusing. She'd worked on it for hours. And he'd just... erased it? Without asking? Without even discussing it first?

Rage flooded through her, instant and volcanic. Her hands shook. Her vision blurred red.

She typed: "You had no right to change my work without asking me."

Derek: "Chill, I was just trying to help."

"I don't need your help. I spent hours on that."

"It's not that deep. Just accept the feedback."

Jasmine wanted to throw her phone across the room. Instead, she typed a paragraph-long response about respect and collaboration and how dare he

Her older brother Caleb walked into her room. "Dinner's whoa, you okay?"

"No, I'm not okay! Derek completely rewrote my work without asking and now he's telling me to 'chill' like I'm being unreasonable!"

"Okay, but like... it's a group project. Sometimes people make changes."

"You don't understand!" The tears came hot and fast. "He dismissed me! He acted like my work was garbage!"

"Jasmine, I think you're overreacting "

"DON'T TELL ME I'M OVERREACTING!" Her voice cracked. She was yelling and crying simultaneously, rage and hurt tangled together so tightly she couldn't separate them.

Caleb backed out of the room, hands raised. "Okay. Sorry. I'll just... tell Mom you'll be down later."

After he left, Jasmine collapsed on her bed, sobbing. She felt out of control. Unhinged. Like her emotions were a wild animal that had broken free and was destroying everything in its path.

And the worst part was knowing even in the moment that her reaction was disproportionate. Derek had been dismissive, yes. Rude, even. But her response? That was disproportionate.

She knew it. And she still couldn't stop it.

That night, her parents knocked on her door.

"We need to talk," her dad said gently.

Jasmine sat up, wiping her eyes. "I know. I freaked out. I'm sorry."

Her mom sat next to her. "Honey, we're worried about you. You've been having these... intense reactions to things lately. More than usual."

"I know. I'm trying to control it. I just " Her voice broke. "I don't know why I'm like this. Why can't I just be normal?"

"You are normal," her dad said. "But I think we need to talk to your doctor. These emotional ups and downs... they're not healthy. You're suffering."

"You think something's wrong with me."

"I think you need more support than you're getting."

Her mom added softly, "When you were diagnosed with ADHD, they mostly talked about focus and hyperactivity. But I've been reading, and... did you know emotional dysregulation is part of ADHD?"

Jasmine looked up. "What?"

"Emotional dysregulation. It's when emotions feel more intense and change more quickly than for neurotypical people. It's a symptom of ADHD that doesn't get talked about much."

Something shifted in Jasmine's chest. "You mean... this isn't just me being dramatic?"

"It's never been you being dramatic. I think it's your ADHD."

Two weeks later, Jasmine sat in Dr. Patel's office a therapist who specialized in ADHD.

"Tell me what's been going on," Dr. Patel said.

Jasmine explained everything. The B+ that felt like failure. The friend hangout that triggered spiraling anxiety. The comma comment that felt like a personal attack. The group project text that sent her into a rage-crying meltdown.

"And everyone tells me I'm overreacting," Jasmine finished. "Which makes me feel even worse because I know they're right. Like, logically I know a B+ is fine and my friend hanging out with someone else doesn't mean she hates me. But it doesn't feel fine. It feels catastrophic."

Dr. Patel nodded. "What you're describing is called emotional dysregulation. It's one of the most common and most overlooked symptoms of ADHD."

"So it's not just me being too sensitive?"

"Not at all. Let me explain what's happening in your brain." Dr. Patel pulled out a diagram. "ADHD affects the prefrontal cortex the part of your brain that regulates emotions. For neurotypical people, emotions escalate gradually. They have time to recognize, process, and respond to feelings. But for people with ADHD, especially with emotional dysregulation, emotions spike suddenly and intensely."

"So I'm not choosing to overreact?"

"You're not overreacting at all. You're having a neurological response. Your brain experiences emotions more intensely and with less ability to modulate them. It's not a character flaw. It's brain wiring."

Jasmine felt tears welling up but this time, relief rather than shame. "Everyone acts like I'm being dramatic on purpose."

"I know. And that's incredibly invalidating. Here's the truth: your emotions are valid. The intensity is real. You're not making it up, and you're not being manipulative. Your brain genuinely experiences a B+ as devastating in the moment, even if your logical brain knows it's fine."

"So what do I do? Just... accept that I'll always be a mess?"

"No. You learn strategies for managing emotional dysregulation. You can't eliminate the intensity that's neurological. But you can develop skills for recognizing escalation earlier, creating space between feeling and reaction, and regulating yourself when emotions spike."

Over the next two months, Jasmine learned what Dr. Patel called "emotional regulation tools."

Tool 1: The Escalation Scale

Dr. Patel taught Jasmine to rate her emotional intensity on a scale of 1-10.

1-3: Calm, manageable 4-6: Feeling it, but can still think clearly 7-8: Strong emotions, harder to think rationally 9-10: Overwhelmed, dysregulated, can't think clearly

The goal wasn't to stop emotions at level 1. The goal was to notice when she hit level 4 or 5 before complete dysregulation and use tools to prevent escalation to 9 or 10.

Jasmine started checking in with herself throughout the day: "Where am I on the scale right now?"

Tool 2: The Pause

When Jasmine felt emotions spiking, Dr. Patel taught her to pause before responding.

Not forever. Just 60 seconds. Just long enough to:

- Name the emotion (I'm feeling rejected/criticized/dismissed)
- Rate the intensity (I'm at a 7 right now)
- Take three deep breaths
- Ask: What do I need right now?

This didn't stop the emotions. But it created a tiny gap between feeling and reacting just enough space to choose her response instead of being hijacked by the emotion.

Tool 3: Physical Regulation

ADHD brains and bodies are connected. When emotions spiked, Jasmine's body went into overdrive heart racing, hands shaking, chest tight. Dr. Patel taught her that calming her body could help calm her emotions.

Strategies:

- Cold water on face or wrists (activates calming nervous system response)
- Vigorous movement (jumping jacks, running, dancing burns off emotional energy)
- Pressure (hugging a pillow, wrapping in a weighted blanket)
- Rhythmic breathing (4 counts in, 6 counts out)

Tool 4: Naming Emotions Specifically

"I'm upset" was too vague. Dr. Patel taught Jasmine to get specific:

- Disappointed (B+ on test)

- Rejected (friend hangout without her)
- Criticized (comma comment)
- Dismissed (group project change)

Naming emotions precisely helped Jasmine's brain process them instead of just drowning in them.

Tool 5: The Thought Challenge

When spiraling into catastrophic thinking (Maya hates me, I'll never succeed, I'm stupid), Jasmine learned to challenge the thoughts:

- What's the evidence for this thought?
- What's the evidence against it?
- What would I tell a friend having this thought?
- What's a more balanced way to think about this?

Not to dismiss her emotions they were real. But to separate intense feelings from distorted thoughts.

Tool 6: Communicating Needs

Jasmine practiced saying:

- "I'm feeling really emotional right now. I need some space to calm down."
- "I'm at a 7 on my emotional scale. Can we talk about this later?"
- "That comment hit me harder than you probably intended. I need a minute."

Advocating for herself instead of either exploding or suppressing everything.

The strategies didn't work immediately. Jasmine still had explosions. Still cried over B+'s. Still spiraled when friends made plans without her.

But slowly, gradually, things started to shift.

In November, Emma mentioned going to a party Jasmine hadn't

been invited to. Jasmine felt the familiar spike that instant conviction that she was being excluded, unwanted, rejected.

But this time, she paused.

Where am I on the scale? 6. Moving toward 7.

What am I feeling? Rejected. Left out.

What's the evidence? Emma mentioned going to a party. That's it. She didn't say "I'm going to this party specifically to exclude you." She just mentioned her plans.

What do I need? To ask instead of assuming.

"Hey," Jasmine said carefully, "I'm feeling kind of left out hearing about this party. Was it, like, a specific invite thing or just a casual mention?"

Emma looked confused. "Oh, it's my cousin's party. Family only. I wasn't even thinking I'm sorry, I should have been clearer."

Just like that, the spiral stopped. Not because the emotion wasn't real Jasmine had genuinely felt rejected. But because she'd paused, named it, and addressed it directly.

In December, Jasmine got an essay back with several critical comments. Her chest tightened. Her eyes burned.

Scale check: 7. Heading toward 8.

Instead of spiraling in class, she asked her teacher if she could take a bathroom break. In the bathroom, she ran cold water over her wrists, took five deep breaths, and named what she was feeling: criticized, ashamed, worried she wasn't good enough.

Then she texted her mom: "Got some tough feedback on my essay. Feeling pretty bad about it. Can we talk later?"

Her mom responded immediately: "Of course, honey. You're doing great. We'll talk after school."

By the time Jasmine got back to class, she was at a 5. Still feeling it, but manageable.

In January, Derek the same Derek from the group project disaster made another dismissive comment about her work. "I don't know, Jasmine's section feels kind of weak."

Jasmine felt the rage start to spike. But this time, she recognized it at level 4.

She took a breath. Paused. Then said calmly, "I'd like to hear specific feedback about what you think needs improvement, rather than a general dismissal of my work."

Derek blinked, surprised. "Uh... okay. I guess I think the conclusion could be stronger?"

"Thanks. I'll work on that."

After class, Maya grabbed her arm. "Dude. That was so mature. Old Jasmine would have exploded at him."

"Old Jasmine didn't have tools," Jasmine said. "New Jasmine is trying really hard not to let her ADHD emotional dysregulation control her life."

"Well, it's working."

It wasn't perfect. Jasmine still had hard days.

In February, she did explode at her brother over something minor he'd borrowed her charger without asking. The anger came so fast and so intense that she couldn't stop it, couldn't pause, couldn't regulate. She yelled. He yelled back. She cried. It was messy.

But afterward, instead of spiraling into shame about being "too sensitive," she apologized and explained: "I have ADHD emotional dysregulation. Sometimes my emotions spike so fast I can't catch them in time. That doesn't make it okay that I yelled at you. I'm working on it."

Caleb, to his credit, said, "Okay. And I should have asked before taking your stuff."

"Yeah, you should have."

They smiled at each other. Not perfect. But honest.

By the end of sophomore year, Jasmine wasn't "cured." She still felt everything intensely. Still got hit by emotional waves that threatened to drown her.

But she had tools now. She had language to explain what was happening. She had strategies that worked more often than not.

And most importantly, she understood: her emotional intensity wasn't a character flaw. It was neurology. It was part of having ADHD. And while it made life harder in some ways, it also made life richer.

She felt joy more intensely too. Felt love more deeply. Felt passion more completely. Her emotional intensity wasn't just a burden it was also a gift.

One afternoon in May, Jasmine sat with Dr. Patel for a check-in session.

"How are you doing?" Dr. Patel asked.

"Better," Jasmine said honestly. "Not perfect. I still have explosions sometimes. But I understand what's happening now. And I have tools."

"That's all we can ask for. You'll always feel things intensely that's how your brain works. But now you're not at the mercy of those feelings. You're learning to work with them."

"Can I ask you something? Will it always be this hard?"

Dr. Patel considered. "It will get easier as you practice these skills. They'll become more automatic. And as you get older, your brain will mature some, which can help with emotional regulation. But yes you'll probably always feel things more intensely than neurotypical people. The question is: do you see that as a curse or a gift?"

Jasmine thought about it. "Both?"

"Good answer."

On the last day of school, Maya asked Jasmine if she wanted to go shopping.

"Just the two of us," Maya added. "Emma's busy."

Two years ago, Jasmine's brain would have immediately gone to: *Why didn't Emma want to come? Is she avoiding me? Does she hate me now?*

But this time, Jasmine just smiled. "Sounds great."

As they walked through the mall, Maya said, "Can I tell you something? You seem... lighter lately. Like, you still feel things a lot that's just you but you don't seem as tortured by it."

"I'm not tortured by it anymore," Jasmine said. "I mean, it's still hard. My emotions are still intense. But I understand why now. It's not a character flaw. It's ADHD emotional dysregulation. And I'm learning how to work with my brain instead of hating it."

"I'm proud of you," Maya said.

Jasmine felt tears prick her eyes but this time, they were happy tears. Good tears. The kind that came with feeling deeply and living authentically.

"Thanks," she said. "Me too."

That night, Jasmine wrote in her journal something Dr. Patel had encouraged.

Dear 15-year-old me from a year ago:

You're not too sensitive. You're not too much. You're not broken.

You have ADHD emotional dysregulation, which means your brain experiences feelings more intensely and quickly than neurotypical brains. That's neurology, not a character flaw.

You're going to learn tools. You're going to get better at recognizing when you're escalating and intervening before you hit 10. You're going to learn to pause, breathe, name your emotions, and communicate your needs.

It won't be perfect. You'll still have explosions sometimes. You'll still cry over things that seem small to other people. You'll still feel everything so, so deeply.

But you'll also understand yourself. You'll have language to explain what's happening. You'll stop apologizing for feeling.

Your emotional intensity is part of you. It makes life harder sometimes, yes. But it also makes life beautiful. You feel joy explosively. You love fiercely. You care deeply.

Don't try to be less. Just learn to navigate the intensity.

You've got this.

Love, 16-year-old you

Jasmine closed the journal and looked at herself in the mirror.

A year ago, she'd seen someone broken. Too emotional. Too sensitive. Too much.

Now she saw someone learning to work with her brain instead of fighting it. Someone who felt deeply and was learning to see that as strength.

She smiled at her reflection.

"You're not too much," she said out loud. "You're exactly right."

And for the first time in her life, she actually believed it.

———

REFLECT

Jasmine's story reveals one of the most challenging and most misunderstood aspects of ADHD: emotional dysregulation. If you've ever been told you're "too sensitive," "too dramatic," or "overreacting" when your emotions feel completely overwhelming and real, this story is for you.

1. **Jasmine described her emotions as going "from zero to one hundred in seconds" with no middle ground. Do you experience this rapid emotional escalation?** What triggers send you from calm to overwhelmed almost instantly?

   ____

   ____

   ____

   ____

2. **A B+ felt catastrophic to Jasmine even though she logically knew it was a good grade. Have you experienced this gap between what you logically know and what you emotionally feel?** What situations trigger emotions that feel disproportionate to the actual event?

---

3. **People constantly told Jasmine she was "overreacting" or "too sensitive," which made her feel even worse. How has this kind of invalidation affected you?** What impact has it had on your self-perception and willingness to express emotions?

---

4. **Jasmine realized she felt multiple emotions simultaneously rage and hurt tangled together during the group project incident. Do you struggle to identify what you're actually feeling when emotions are intense?** How does emotional overwhelm make it harder to name specific feelings?

---

5. **Learning that emotional dysregulation was a symptom of ADHD, not a character flaw, changed everything for Jasmine. If you experience intense emotions, how does it feel to learn this is neurological rather than you being "too much"?** What shifts when you reframe emotional intensity as brain wiring rather than personal failing?

____

____

____

____

6. **Jasmine had to learn to recognize escalation at level 4-5 before reaching 9-10 dysregulation. Do you have a sense of your emotional escalation pattern?** Can you identify early warning signs, or do emotions hit you all at once?

____

____

____

____

7. **Jasmine's emotional intensity applied to positive emotions too she felt joy and love more deeply. Do you experience this full spectrum of emotional intensity?** How might your emotional sensitivity be both challenge and gift?

____

____

____

____

8. **By the end, Jasmine stopped apologizing for feeling and started advocating for her needs. What would it look like for you to stop apologizing for your emotional intensity and start communicating what you need when emotions spike?**

____

____

____

ACT

This week, learn to catch emotional escalation early and use physical regulation tools before you reach explosion.

ADHD emotional dysregulation means your emotions spike from 0 to 100 with almost no middle ground, and the intensity feels overwhelming and real. You're not "too sensitive" you have a neurological difference in how your brain processes emotional intensity. Your task is to recognize your personal escalation pattern and interrupt it before you reach full dysregulation.

Build your personal "Escalation Scale" and regulation toolkit:

For three days, track every emotional spike (anger, anxiety, rejection, frustration, overwhelm):

- What was the trigger?
- What did you feel physically? (chest tight, face hot, hands shaking, stomach dropping, etc.)
- What number would you rate it (1-10)?
- How quickly did you go from calm to intense?

After three days, identify your personal early warning signs. Most people have physical cues at level 4-5 before hitting 9-10 explosion. Common early signs: slight tension in chest, starting to feel warm, jaw tightening, hands clenching, breathing getting faster.

Now practice "The Pause" this week: When you notice early warning signs (4-5 level), use ONE physical regulation technique IMMEDIATELY:

- **Cold water:** Splash face, run over wrists, hold ice
- **Movement:** Jumping jacks, run in place, dance for 2 minutes
- **Pressure:** Tight hug, weighted blanket, push hands together hard
- **Breathing:** 4 counts in, 6 counts out, repeat 5 times

The key is catching it EARLY (at 4-5) before you hit 8-9 where regulation is much harder. Physical regulation techniques work because they activate your parasympathetic nervous system (body's calming response).

Important reminders:

- Emotional dysregulation is neurological you're not "overreacting," you're having a brain-based response
- The pain of emotional spikes is REAL even when the trigger seems small to others
- Catching escalation at 4-5 is much easier than trying to calm down from 9-10
- Physical regulation works better than trying to "think your way" out of dysregulation
- You'll still have explosions while learning that's normal, just practice repair after
- Feelings aren't facts intense emotion doesn't mean accurate perception of the situation
- Emotional intensity is also your gift you feel joy, love, excitement, passion deeply too
- People who call you "too sensitive" don't understand ADHD emotional dysregulation

STORY 5: THE REJECTION ECHO

A STORY about learning that the pain of rejection isn't about weakness it's about a brain that feels emotional pain more intensely, and you can learn to reality-check before the spiral takes over.

Jordan Hayes stared at the note his history teacher had handed him at the end of class.

Jordan - I noticed you didn't turn in your history project. Please see me after class tomorrow to discuss. - Ms. Martinez

His stomach dropped. His chest tightened. Heat flooded his face.

She hated him. She thought he was lazy and irresponsible. She was disappointed in him. She probably told the other teachers about him. They probably all talked about what a failure he was in the teacher's lounge.

Jordan's hands shook as he folded the note and shoved it in his pocket. His mind spiraled through every interaction he'd had with Ms. Martinez this semester. Had she always disliked him? That time she'd asked him to stop talking in class was she singling him out? The B- on his last essay was that her way of telling him he wasn't good enough?

The rejection felt physical. Like a weight on his chest. Like his lungs had forgotten how to work.

It was just a note about a missing assignment. Jordan knew that intellectually.

But it didn't feel like "just" anything. It felt like the end of the world.

Jordan had ADHD. Combined type, diagnosed in eighth grade after years of teachers commenting that he was "bright but unfocused" and "needs to apply himself more." The diagnosis helped explain some things the difficulty starting tasks, the constant fidgeting, the way his mind wandered even when he was trying to pay attention.

But the ADHD diagnosis didn't explain why rejection felt like being stabbed.

A teacher's mild criticism didn't just sting it felt like proof that he was fundamentally inadequate and would never succeed.

A friend not responding to a text didn't just annoy him it triggered instant panic that he'd said something wrong and the friendship was over.

A girl saying she was busy when he asked her to hang out didn't feel like a scheduling conflict it felt like personal rejection, confirmation that he was unlikeable and would be alone forever.

His brain amplified every perceived rejection into catastrophic emotional pain. And the worst part? The rejection didn't even have to be real. His brain found it everywhere, in every neutral interaction, every delayed response, every slight change in someone's tone.

Eleventh grade started with Jordan making a promise to himself: this year would be different. He'd try harder. He'd put himself out there. He'd stop hiding.

That lasted exactly three weeks.

In September, Jordan worked up the courage to audition for the school play. He loved theater had done drama club in middle school but had been too afraid to try out in high school. Too much risk of rejection.

But this year was supposed to be different. So he auditioned.

He thought it went okay. Not great, but okay. He'd remembered his lines, projected his voice, made some decent choices.

Two days later, the cast list went up.

Jordan's name wasn't on it.

He stood in the hallway, staring at the list, feeling like someone had reached into his chest and crushed his heart. Around him, students celebrated. "I got Mercutio!" "I'm Lady Macbeth!" Laughter, excitement, joy.

Jordan felt like he was drowning.

It wasn't just disappointment. It was shame. Humiliation. Proof that he wasn't good enough, would never be good enough, should never have tried in the first place.

The theater teacher, Mr. Chen, approached him. "Hey Jordan, I'm sorry you didn't get cast this time. You had a solid audition. It was really competitive."

Jordan managed to nod, but all he heard was: *You weren't good enough. Everyone else was better. You failed.*

"I hope you'll try again next semester," Mr. Chen continued.

Translation: He's being nice because he feels sorry for me. He knows I'm terrible.

Jordan left school early that day, claiming he felt sick. It wasn't a lie the rejection made him physically nauseated.

At home, he lay in bed, replaying the audition in his mind. Every mistake magnified. Every weak moment highlighted. He'd been so stupid to think he could do this.

His phone buzzed. His friend Marcus: *Dude did you hear I got Benvolio?? Want to come celebrate?*

Jordan turned off his phone. He couldn't celebrate. He couldn't be around other people's success when he was drowning in his own failure.

October brought more rejection real and imagined.

Jordan asked his crush, Emily, if she wanted to study together for their upcoming chemistry test.

"Oh, I'm actually studying with Sophia," Emily said. "But thanks for asking!"

Neutral response. Polite. Reasonable.

But Jordan's brain translated it as: *She doesn't want to spend time with you. She'd rather be with Sophia. You're not even a consideration.*

He spent the rest of the day convinced that Emily found him annoying, that she'd probably told Sophia about his awkward invitation, that they were probably laughing about him right now.

A week later, his English teacher handed back essays with comments. Jordan got a B with a note: "Good analysis, but your thesis could be stronger."

Constructive feedback. Helpful, even.

But Jordan read it as: *Your work is mediocre. You're not as smart as you think you are. She's disappointed in you.*

He couldn't focus for the rest of class, too busy spiraling through shame and inadequacy.

That weekend, Marcus invited him to a party. Jordan almost said yes, but then anxiety kicked in. What if he showed up and nobody wanted to talk to him? What if he said something stupid? What if people were only inviting him out of pity? What if he went and realized nobody actually liked him?

Better not to go. Better to avoid the possibility of rejection altogether.

"Can't make it," Jordan texted Marcus. "Family stuff."

Marcus responded: "K"

Just "K." Not "okay, no problem!" or "maybe next time!" Just "K."

Jordan stared at the single letter, his stomach churning. Marcus was mad at him. Marcus was tired of him flaking. Marcus probably didn't even want to be friends anymore.

He almost texted an explanation, an apology, but what would he even say? *Sorry I'm so anxious about rejection that I can't go to parties?* That would just make Marcus think he was weird.

Better to say nothing.

By November, Jordan had withdrawn almost completely.

He stopped trying out for things. Stopped asking people to hang out. Stopped raising his hand in class even when he knew the answer. Stopped putting any effort into assignments that would be graded subjectively because the possibility of criticism was unbearable.

His mom noticed. "You've been really quiet lately. Everything okay?"

"Fine," Jordan said automatically.

"You haven't had friends over in weeks. What happened to Marcus?"

"Nothing. We're fine."

"Jordan." Her voice was gentle but firm. "Talk to me."

And suddenly, unexpectedly, Jordan's eyes filled with tears. "I just... I can't handle it, okay? I can't handle people not liking me. I can't handle trying and failing. I can't handle criticism or rejection or any of it. It hurts too much."

His mom sat next to him. "What do you mean it hurts too much?"

"Like... physically. Like someone's punching me in the chest. Like I can't breathe." He wiped his eyes, embarrassed. "I know it's stupid. I know I'm overreacting. But I can't stop it."

"It's not stupid. And I don't think you're overreacting." She paused. "Have you heard of rejection sensitive dysphoria?"

Jordan shook his head.

"It's something that often goes with ADHD. It's when rejection or even perceived rejection causes intense emotional pain. Not just hurt feelings. Actual, physical, overwhelming pain."

Jordan looked at her. "That's... that's a real thing?"

"Very real. Let me show you."

She pulled up articles on her phone. Jordan read, his hands shaking slightly.

Rejection Sensitive Dysphoria (RSD) is extreme emotional pain triggered by the perception real or imagined of being rejected, criticized, or failing to meet expectations.

People with RSD describe the pain as "unbearable," "devastating," "like being stabbed."

RSD can cause people to avoid situations where rejection is possible, even when those situations could be positive.

Many people with RSD misinterpret neutral interactions as rejection or criticism.

Every sentence felt like it was describing his exact experience.

"This is me," Jordan whispered. "This is exactly what I feel."

"I know, honey. I've watched you struggle with this for years. I didn't have a name for it until recently."

"So I'm not just weak? I'm not just too sensitive?"

"Not at all. It's neurological. Your ADHD brain feels rejection more intensely than neurotypical brains do. The pain is real."

For the first time in months, Jordan felt something other than shame. Relief. Validation. Understanding.

"Can it be fixed?"

"It can be managed. Let's talk to your doctor."

Two weeks later, Jordan sat in Dr. Kim's office his psychiatrist who managed his ADHD medication.

"Tell me about the rejection sensitivity," Dr. Kim said.

Jordan explained everything. The play audition that sent him spiraling for days. The text from his teacher that felt like devastating criticism. The friend's "K" that convinced him the friendship was over. The constant avoidance of anything that might result in rejection.

Dr. Kim listened carefully. "What you're describing is classic RSD. It's one of the most painful aspects of ADHD, and one of the least talked about."

"Why doesn't anyone talk about it?"

"Partially because it doesn't fit the stereotype of ADHD being about hyperactivity and focus. Partially because people with RSD often hide it they're so ashamed of how intensely they feel rejection that they don't tell anyone."

Jordan nodded. That was exactly what he'd been doing.

"Here's what's happening in your brain," Dr. Kim continued. "ADHD affects emotional regulation. For people with RSD, the brain interprets rejection or potential rejection as a threat. It triggers a fight-or-flight response. The emotional pain is as real as physical pain."

"So when my teacher texted me about a missing assignment and I felt like I was dying... that was real?"

"Completely real. Your brain perceived that text as criticism, which triggered RSD, which caused actual emotional and physical distress."

"How do I make it stop?"

"You can't eliminate RSD it's part of your ADHD neurology. But you can learn to recognize it, reality-check your perceptions, and prevent avoidance patterns from taking over your life."

Dr. Kim taught Jordan what he called "RSD management strategies."

Strategy 1: Name it when it happens

When Jordan felt that familiar crushing pain, instead of spiraling, he needed to pause and think: *This might be RSD. My brain is interpreting something as rejection and amplifying the pain.*

Naming it didn't stop the pain, but it created a tiny bit of distance just enough to question whether the rejection was real.

Strategy 2: Reality-check before spiraling

When convinced someone was rejecting him, Jordan learned to ask:

- What actually happened? (Just facts, no interpretation)
- What did I interpret it to mean?
- What's the evidence for my interpretation?
- What are other possible explanations?

Strategy 3: Separate pain from reality

The pain was real. But that didn't mean the rejection was real.

Jordan needed to learn: *I'm feeling intense pain right now. That's valid. But feelings aren't facts.*

Strategy 4: Reach out instead of withdrawing

RSD made Jordan want to hide, avoid, disconnect. Dr. Kim taught him to do the opposite when he felt rejected, tell someone.

"I'm feeling really rejected right now, even though I'm not sure if that's what actually happened."

Being vulnerable about RSD reduced its power.

Strategy 5: Build evidence against RSD lies

RSD told Jordan constant lies: Nobody likes you. You're not good enough. They're all talking about you. Dr. Kim had him create a list of "RSD lie evidence" concrete facts that contradicted the lies.

- Marcus invites me to hang out regularly
- My parents love me
- Teachers have said positive things about my work
- I have friends who text me first
- Emily smiled at me in the hallway yesterday

When RSD whispered that nobody liked him, Jordan could reference the list.

Strategy 6: Medication adjustment

Dr. Kim explained that some people found their RSD improved with medication adjustments. They discussed whether changing his ADHD medication dose or adding something to help with emotional regulation might help.

They decided to try a slight increase in his stimulant medication. It wasn't specifically for RSD, but better ADHD management sometimes reduced emotional dysregulation, including RSD.

Jordan started implementing the strategies, though it was harder than he expected.

When Marcus texted "K" and Jordan's brain screamed *He hates you now,* Jordan forced himself to pause.

This is RSD. What actually happened? Marcus said 'K' in response to me canceling. What do I think it means? That he's mad and doesn't want to be friends. Evidence? Literally just the letter K. Other explanations? He was busy. He was driving. He didn't think a longer response was necessary. He's fine with it.

Jordan texted back: "Sorry for flaking. Want to hang out this weekend?"

Marcus responded immediately: "Yeah man! Let's hit the arcade."

The friendship wasn't over. The rejection wasn't real. RSD had lied.

In December, Jordan decided to try something terrifying: ask Emily to the winter formal.

Every part of him wanted to avoid it. The possibility of rejection was overwhelming. His RSD brain screamed at him: *Don't do it. She'll say no. You'll be humiliated. Everyone will know you got rejected. It's not worth the risk.*

But Dr. Kim's words echoed: *RSD can't control your life unless you let it. The pain of avoidance is often worse than the pain of actual rejection.*

Jordan found Emily after school. His hands were shaking. His heart was pounding.

"Hey Emily, I was wondering... would you want to go to winter formal with me?"

Emily smiled. "Oh, that's really sweet. I'm actually already going with my friend group we're all going together. But thanks for asking!"

She walked away. Jordan stood there, bracing for the crushing devastation, the overwhelming pain, the proof that he was unlikeable and should never have tried.

But... it didn't come. Not like before.

He felt disappointed, yes. A little embarrassed. But not destroyed. Not crushed.

Because he'd reality-checked it immediately: *She said no to going as a date, but she said it sweetly. She mentioned she's going with friends not that she doesn't want to go with me specifically. She thanked me for asking. This wasn't cruel rejection. This was just incompatible plans.*

Jordan texted his mom: "Asked Emily to formal. She said no. I'm okay."

His mom responded: "I'm so proud of you for trying. That took courage."

And weirdly, Jordan felt proud too. He'd asked despite the RSD fear. He'd survived the "no." The world hadn't ended.

In January, Jordan did something even braver: he auditioned for the spring play.

The RSD resistance was intense. *You failed last time. You'll fail again. Why subject yourself to that pain?*

But Jordan recognized it now. *That's RSD talking. Last time wasn't failure it was just not getting cast. And even if I don't get cast this time, I'll survive. The avoidance is worse than the risk.*

He auditioned. This time, he didn't spend days spiraling afterward. He acknowledged he might not get cast, and that would sting, but it wouldn't destroy him.

When the cast list went up, his name was on it. Small role, but there.

Jordan stared at his name, feeling something he hadn't felt in months: pride. Not because he'd gotten cast though that was great but because he'd tried despite the RSD fear.

February brought a bigger challenge: group presentation in history class.

Jordan's group met to divide up tasks. One group member, Tyler, said, "Jordan, maybe you should handle the slides since your writing skills aren't as strong."

Old Jordan would have heard: *You're not smart enough to write. We don't trust you. You're the weak link.*

New Jordan paused. *Is this RSD or real feedback?*

He asked: "Hey Tyler, what makes you think my writing skills aren't strong?"

Tyler looked confused. "What? I didn't say that. I said maybe you should do slides since you're good at visual stuff. You made that really cool infographic for the last project."

Oh.

Jordan had completely misinterpreted. Tyler wasn't saying he was bad at writing he was saying he was good at design.

"Sorry, I misunderstood. Yeah, I can do the slides."

After the meeting, Jordan texted Dr. Kim: "Just caught myself misinterpreting a compliment as criticism. RSD tried to get me but I reality-checked it."

Dr. Kim responded: "That's exactly the skill. Well done."

By spring, Jordan wasn't "cured" of RSD. He still felt rejection intensely. Still had moments where the pain overwhelmed him.

But he had tools now. He could recognize RSD when it hit. Could reality-check before spiraling. Could reach out instead of withdrawing.

Most importantly, he'd stopped letting RSD control his life through avoidance.

He tried out for the talent show didn't make it, felt disappointed, survived.

He asked three different people to hang out one said yes, two were busy. He didn't interpret the "busy" as rejection.

He turned in an essay knowing it might get criticized it did, and it hurt, but he used the feedback to improve rather than spiraling into shame.

One afternoon in May, Marcus asked him, "What happened to you this year? You seem... different. Like, more confident or something."

Jordan considered how to explain. "I learned I have something called rejection sensitive dysphoria. It's part of ADHD. It makes rejection feel like being stabbed, even when the rejection isn't real. I was avoiding everything because I couldn't handle the pain."

"Damn. That sounds awful."

"It is. But I learned how to manage it. I can't control the pain, but I can control whether I let it stop me from trying."

"That's actually really brave, man."

Jordan smiled. A year ago, he would've interpreted that compliment as pity or sarcasm. Now he could just... accept it.

"Thanks. It doesn't feel brave. It feels like survival."

"Same thing sometimes."

On the last day of junior year, Jordan's history teacher the one whose text had triggered a complete meltdown back in September asked him to stay after class.

Jordan's RSD immediately activated. *You're in trouble. She's disappointed. You failed.*

But he reality-checked it. *This is RSD. Wait for actual information.*

Ms. Martinez smiled. "I wanted to tell you I've really seen growth in you this semester. Your last few assignments have been excellent, and you've been more engaged in class discussions. Whatever you're doing, keep it up."

Jordan felt his eyes sting with tears. Not pain this time something else. Relief. Validation. Pride.

"Thank you," he managed. "That means a lot."

Walking out of school that day, Jordan thought about the text from September that had sent him spiraling. *Please see me after class to discuss.* He'd been so convinced it meant she hated him.

It had just been about a missing assignment.

That was the thing about RSD it took neutral or even positive things and translated them into rejection. But with practice, Jordan was learning to recognize the translation errors. To pause. To reality-check. To ask for clarification instead of assuming the worst.

That summer, Jordan volunteered at a theater camp for kids. On the first day, the camp director gave feedback on his teaching demo. "Great energy, but try to project your voice more so kids in the back can hear."

A year ago, Jordan would've heard: *You're terrible at this. You're failing. You shouldn't be here.*

But now, he heard what was actually said: constructive feedback about volume. Not rejection. Not criticism of his worth. Just helpful information.

"Got it, I'll work on that," Jordan said.

And he did.

On the last night of camp, one of the kids, a shy eight-year-old named Max, said, "Jordan, you're my favorite counselor."

Jordan felt the warmth spread through his chest real connection, real appreciation. For so long, RSD had convinced him that nobody genuinely liked him, that any positive feedback was pity or obligation.

But this was real. This kid actually liked him. And Jordan could feel it without RSD distorting it.

"Thanks, Max. You did great this week."

Later, Jordan texted Dr. Kim: "Had a moment today where I received a compliment and just... accepted it. Didn't analyze it. Didn't assume it was fake. Just felt good."

Dr. Kim: "That's major progress. That's what managing RSD looks like not eliminating the sensitivity, but learning to separate real from perceived rejection."

The night before senior year started, Jordan journaled something Dr. Kim had recommended.

Things I know now that I didn't know a year ago:

1. RSD is real. The pain I feel isn't weakness or overreaction it's neurology.

2. Feelings aren't facts. I can feel rejected without actually being rejected.

3. Reality-checking works. Pause, ask questions, gather evidence.

4. Avoidance makes RSD worse. The more I avoid, the more power RSD has.

5. People usually aren't rejecting me. Most of the time, they're just busy, distracted, or communicating neutrally.

6. When someone does reject me, I can survive it. Rejection hurts, but it doesn't destroy me.

7. Trying is braver than hiding.

8. I'm not alone in this. RSD is common with ADHD. Other people feel this too.

Jordan closed the journal and looked at himself in the mirror.

A year ago, he'd seen someone too sensitive, too weak to handle normal life. Someone who needed to hide to survive.

Now he saw someone who felt things intensely but who was learning to work with that intensity instead of being controlled by it.

The rejection would still hurt. The RSD would still flare up. But it wouldn't run his life anymore.

Jordan smiled at his reflection.

"Senior year," he said out loud. "Let's do this."

And for the first time in a long time, he actually believed he could.

———

REFLECT

Jordan's story captures one of the most painful and least-discussed aspects of ADHD: Rejection Sensitive Dysphoria (RSD). If you've ever felt devastating emotional pain from criticism, perceived rejection, or even neutral interactions pain so intense it feels physical this story is for you.

1. **Jordan described rejection as feeling "like being stabbed" or "like someone punching him in the chest." Do you experience rejection this intensely?** How would you describe the physical sensation of rejection or criticism for you?

   ____

   ____

   ____

   ____

2. **Jordan misinterpreted many neutral interactions as rejection: Emily's scheduling conflict, Tyler's comment**

about visual skills, Marcus's "K" text. **Do you find yourself reading rejection into neutral situations?** What patterns do you notice do certain types of interactions trigger RSD more than others?

____

____

____

____

3. **When Jordan didn't make the play cast, he interpreted it as "proof he wasn't good enough and should never have tried." Does rejection feel like evidence of your fundamental inadequacy?** How does RSD affect your willingness to try new things or put yourself out there?

____

____

____

____

4. **Jordan's RSD led him to avoid anything where rejection was possible he stopped trying out for things, stopped asking people to hang out, stopped raising his hand in class. What has RSD-driven avoidance cost you?** What opportunities have you missed because the possibility of rejection felt unbearable?

____

____

____

____

5. **Learning that RSD was a neurological symptom of ADHD, not a character flaw, changed everything for Jordan. If you experience intense rejection sensitivity,**

how does it feel to learn this is brain wiring rather than you being "too sensitive" or "weak"? What shifts when you reframe RSD as a symptom rather than a personality problem?

____
____
____
____

6. **Jordan had to learn that "feelings aren't facts" he could feel intensely rejected without actually being rejected. How difficult is it for you to separate the intensity of your feelings from the reality of the situation?** When emotions are overwhelming, can you still reality-check?

____
____
____
____

7. **Jordan built a list of "RSD lie evidence" concrete facts that contradicted RSD's constant narrative that nobody liked him. What "lies" does your RSD tell you consistently?** (Examples: "Nobody actually likes you," "They're just being nice out of pity," "You're always the problem," "Everyone's talking about you")

____
____
____
____

8. **By the end, Jordan could receive a compliment and just accept it without analyzing or assuming it was fake. Do you struggle to accept positive feedback**

because RSD tells you it can't be real? What would it feel like to trust that people genuinely like and appreciate you?

____

____

____

____

ACT

This week, practice reality-checking perceived rejection before spiraling into RSD.

Rejection Sensitive Dysphoria (RSD) means your ADHD brain interprets neutral interactions as rejection and amplifies emotional pain to crushing levels. The pain is real, but the rejection often isn't. Your task is to create a gap between feeling rejected and believing the rejection is real to reality-check before spiraling.

Practice "The RSD Reality-Check Protocol" every time you feel rejected:

This week, when you feel that familiar crushing rejection pain (chest tight, convinced someone hates you, spiraling about what you did wrong), PAUSE and answer these questions on paper or in your phone:

1. **What actually happened?** (Just facts: "Friend said they're busy this weekend")
2. **What am I interpreting it to mean?** (Your RSD story: "They don't want to hang out with me, they're tired of me, they're probably hanging out with others")
3. **What's the EVIDENCE for my interpretation?** (Usually just: the one thing that happened)
4. **What's evidence AGAINST my interpretation?** (They've invited me before, they texted me yesterday, they suggested next weekend instead)
5. **What are OTHER possible explanations?** (They actually are busy, they have family obligations, this has nothing to do with me)

6. **Most likely reality?** (They're probably just busy, not rejecting me)

Do this BEFORE texting apologies, withdrawing, making assumptions, or acting on the rejection feeling. The reality-check doesn't stop the pain (RSD will still hurt), but it prevents you from making decisions based on a rejection that isn't real.

Also, reach out instead of withdrawing. When you feel rejected, your instinct is to hide. Do the opposite: "Hey, my brain is telling me you're upset with me because [X]. Is that true, or is this just my RSD being dramatic?" Most of the time, you'll find the rejection wasn't real.

Important reminders:

- RSD pain is REAL even when the rejection isn't you're not making it up or exaggerating
- Your ADHD brain interprets neutral interactions as rejection that's neurology, not accurate perception
- Most of the time, people aren't rejecting you they're busy, distracted, or communicating neutrally
- Reality-checking doesn't stop the pain, but it prevents you from acting on false perceptions
- Feelings aren't facts intense rejection pain doesn't mean you're actually being rejected
- Reaching out is braver than withdrawing vulnerability reduces RSD's power
- Build a list of "RSD lies" and evidence against them to reference when spiraling
- Medication adjustments sometimes help RSD talk to your prescriber if it's severe

CHAPTER 6

STORY 6: THE MEDICATION DECISION

A STORY about making your own informed choice about ADHD medication and learning that support tools don't change who you are, they help you become more fully yourself.

Riley Foster sat in Dr. Chen's office, the ADHD diagnosis still sinking in. She'd suspected for months done the research, taken the screeners, recognized herself in every symptom list. But hearing it officially felt different. More real. More permanent.

"So," Dr. Chen said gently, "now that we've confirmed the diagnosis, let's talk about treatment options."

Riley's mom leaned forward, pen poised over her notebook. Her dad sat back, arms crossed, jaw tight.

"There are several approaches," Dr. Chen continued. "Behavioral strategies, organizational systems, accommodations at school. And for many people, medication is also part of the treatment plan."

Riley felt her stomach clench. She'd known this was coming. ADHD medication. Stimulants. Pills that would... what? Change her? Fix her? Make her someone different?

"What kind of medication?" her mom asked.

"Stimulant medications are first-line treatment for ADHD. They help the prefrontal cortex the brain's executive function center work more efficiently. We'd start with a low dose and adjust as needed."

"Side effects?" her dad asked, his voice sharp.

"Common ones include decreased appetite, trouble sleeping initially, sometimes headaches. Most side effects are mild and improve as the body adjusts. We monitor closely."

Riley watched her parents. Her mom was nodding, taking notes. Her dad looked skeptical, almost angry.

"I'd like Riley to think about whether she wants to try medication," Dr. Chen said, turning to her. "This is your decision. I can provide information, but ultimately, you get to choose what feels right."

Riley's throat felt tight. "Can I think about it?"

"Absolutely. Take your time. Do research. Ask questions. There's no rush."

In the car ride home, the silence was heavy.

Finally, Riley's dad spoke. "You're not taking those pills."

"Dan " her mom started.

"I'm serious, Michelle. Those are serious drugs. They're basically speed. They're overprescribed to kids who just need more discipline."

"The doctor said they're safe "

"Doctors say lots of things. I've read about kids becoming zombies on that stuff. Losing their personality. Getting addicted."

Riley stared out the window, her chest tight. She hadn't even decided if she wanted medication, and already there was a fight.

"It's Riley's choice," her mom said firmly. "The doctor said she gets to decide."

"She's fifteen. She can't make a decision like this."

"Then we help her research and make an informed choice. We don't just shut it down."

Riley wished she could disappear. Or hyperfocus on something else. Or be anywhere but trapped in this car between her arguing parents.

That night, Riley did what she always did when overwhelmed: research.

She opened her laptop and typed: "ADHD medication teens experiences."

The results were... confusing. Some articles called stimulants "miracle drugs" that changed lives. Others warned about dangerous side effects, addiction potential, stunted growth. Some people said medication was essential. Others said it was unnecessary and overused.

How was she supposed to know what to believe?

Riley found a Reddit thread: "Teens on ADHD meds - tell me your honest experience."

She read for two hours.

Some responses made medication sound amazing:

- *"Changed my life. I can actually finish things now."*
- *"Like putting on glasses for the first time. Suddenly the world was clear."*
- *"I'm still me, just... more functional."*

Others were more cautious:

- *"Helped my focus but killed my appetite. Lost 15 pounds in two months."*
- *"Made me feel flat emotionally. Like all my feelings were dimmed."*
- *"Works great but I hate being dependent on a pill."*

And some were negative:

- *"Made me feel like a robot. Couldn't be creative anymore."*
- *"Side effects weren't worth it for me."*

Riley closed her laptop, more confused than before.

The next day at school, Riley found her friend Asha at lunch.

"Can I ask you something kind of personal?" Riley said.

"Always."

"You take ADHD medication, right?"

Asha nodded. "Since seventh grade. Why?"

"I just got diagnosed. Doctor suggested trying medication. I'm... scared, I guess. What's it like?"

Asha considered. "Honestly? It helps a lot. But it's not magic. And there were side effects at first I wasn't hungry and had trouble sleeping. But we adjusted the dose and those got better."

"Does it change who you are?"

"That's what I was afraid of too. My dad said the same thing worried I'd lose my personality. But no. I'm still me. I still make jokes, I still love art, I still get excited about things. I just... don't lose my backpack five times a week anymore. And I can actually finish my homework in reasonable time."

"So it's worth it?"

"For me, yeah. But everyone's different. My cousin tried medication and hated it made her feel anxious. She does fine without it, just uses a lot of systems and accommodations."

Riley felt slightly better. At least it wasn't all-or-nothing.

At dinner that night, Riley's parents were still divided.

"I made an appointment with our family doctor," her dad announced. "To get a second opinion."

"She already got evaluated by a specialist," Riley's mom said.

"I want another opinion before we start drugging our daughter."

"*Treating,*" her mom corrected. "Not drugging. Treating a medical condition."

"It's not a medical condition. It's a behavioral issue. She just needs better study habits."

Riley dropped her fork. "Dad, I have ADHD. It's diagnosed. It's real."

"I know you're struggling, honey. But there are other ways to handle it besides pills."

"Like what? Try harder? I've been trying my whole life. I try so hard I'm exhausted all the time and I still can't keep up."

Her dad's expression softened. "I just don't want you to change. You're creative and funny and spontaneous. I don't want medication to take that away."

Riley felt tears burn behind her eyes. "What if medication doesn't take it away? What if it helps me actually USE those things instead of being too scattered to finish anything?"

Silence.

Her mom reached across the table and squeezed Riley's hand. "We'll figure it out. Together."

The next week, Riley went to the second opinion appointment with their family doctor, Dr. Ramirez.

Her dad asked pointed questions: "Aren't stimulants addictive?" "What about long-term effects?" "Can't she just use coping strategies instead?"

Dr. Ramirez answered patiently. "Stimulants prescribed for ADHD, at therapeutic doses, are not addictive. Research shows they actually reduce the risk of substance abuse later people with untreated ADHD are more likely to self-medicate. Long-term studies show ADHD medications are safe when properly monitored. And yes, coping strategies are important but they work better when the brain's executive function is supported by medication."

"So you're saying she needs medication?"

"I'm saying it's an option that helps many people. It's not mandatory. But it's a legitimate treatment for a neurological condition."

Riley appreciated that Dr. Ramirez didn't push. Just provided information.

After the appointment, her dad was quiet.

Finally, he said, "If you want to try it, I won't stop you. But I want you to really think about it. Not just because a doctor suggested it."

Riley nodded. "I will."

Riley spent the next two weeks researching everything she could find:

She read medical studies about ADHD medication efficacy and safety.

She watched YouTube videos of people sharing their experiences.

She joined an online ADHD community and asked questions.

She talked to her school counselor, who said many students found medication helpful but emphasized it was a personal choice.

She made a pros and cons list:

PROS:

- Might help me focus better
- Could make schoolwork less exhausting
- Might reduce constant mental fog
- Could help me finish things I start
- Would support the accommodations and strategies I'm building

CONS:

- Side effects (appetite, sleep, unknown)
- Scared of changing who I am
- Worried about dependency
- Uncomfortable with taking a pill every day

- Pressure from both sides (mom pushing yes, dad pushing no)

Looking at the list, Riley realized: her biggest fear wasn't actually the medication itself. It was making the wrong choice. Disappointing someone. Making a decision she'd regret.

Riley made an appointment to talk to Dr. Chen again, this time without her parents.

"I've been researching medication," Riley said. "I think I want to try it. But I'm scared."

"What scares you most?"

"That it'll change who I am. That I'll become... I don't know, robotic or boring or not me anymore."

Dr. Chen nodded. "That's a very common fear. Here's what I can tell you: ADHD medication doesn't change your personality. It helps your brain's executive function system work more efficiently. Think of it like glasses they don't change who you are, they help you see more clearly."

"But some people say they felt different on medication."

"Some people do feel different but usually they describe feeling more like themselves, not less. The ADHD symptoms were masking their true personality. When those symptoms are managed, they can be who they actually are."

"What if I don't like it?"

"Then you stop. Medication isn't permanent. If you try it and it doesn't work for you whether because of side effects or just not helping you can stop taking it. This isn't a lifetime commitment. It's an experiment to see if it helps."

That made Riley feel better. Not permanent. Just trying.

"What if I try it and it does help? Am I going to need it forever?"

"Some people take ADHD medication long-term. Some people use it situationally like during school but not summer. Some people try it for a while, build better strategies, and eventually manage without it. There's no one right path."

"Okay," Riley said slowly. "I think I want to try."

Riley's mom was thrilled. Her dad was resigned but supportive. They agreed to try medication for one month, with close monitoring, and then reassess.

Dr. Chen prescribed a low dose of a stimulant medication. Riley would take it every morning.

"Keep a journal," Dr. Chen suggested. "Track how you feel, what changes you notice, any side effects. That'll help us adjust if needed."

Riley started the medication on a Saturday morning. That way if something went wrong, she wouldn't be at school.

She took the small pill, then waited.

Nothing happened.

An hour later, still nothing. She felt exactly the same.

Maybe it doesn't work for me, she thought.

But then, around 10:30 AM, Riley sat down to finish homework she'd been avoiding for days. She opened her laptop to write an essay for English.

And she... started writing.

Not reluctantly. Not forcing herself. She just started. The words came. Her thoughts organized themselves. She wrote a paragraph, then another, then another.

Two hours later, she'd finished the entire essay. First draft, complete.

Riley stared at her laptop in disbelief.

It usually took her six hours to write an essay lots of staring at blank pages, getting distracted, starting over, losing her train of thought. This had taken two hours and felt... easy? Not effortless, but normal. Like how other people probably wrote essays.

She checked the essay. It was good. Coherent. Organized. She'd actually followed her outline instead of forgetting it halfway through.

Riley grabbed her journal and wrote:

Day 1: I think the medication is working? I wrote my whole essay without stopping every five minutes. This is what focus feels like??? Is this how neurotypical people feel all the time?

The first week on medication was an adjustment.

Day 2: Riley noticed she wasn't hungry at lunch. Forced herself to eat half a sandwich. Made a note: *Appetite definitely decreased. Need to remember to eat.*

Day 3: Focused well in school. Took notes in history class without zoning out. Actually remembered what the teacher said. Stayed up late because she wasn't tired at normal bedtime. Note: *Trouble sleeping. Took pill too late? Need to take it earlier.*

Day 4: Took medication at 7 AM instead of 8:30 AM. Slept better that night. Ate breakfast before pill kicked in. Better day overall.

Day 5: Had a small headache in afternoon as medication wore off. Drank water, felt better. Noticed the "fog" came back around 4 PM when medication wore off completely. That was weird she'd never noticed the fog before because it was just... always there.

Weekend: Riley experimented with not taking medication on Saturday. Immediately noticed the difference. Couldn't focus on homework. Started five different projects, finished none. Took medication on Sunday, finished projects she'd started Saturday.

By the end of the first month, Riley had adjusted to the medication. The side effects had mostly resolved she'd learned to eat breakfast before her appetite decreased, take the medication early enough that it wore off before bedtime, stay hydrated to prevent headaches.

More importantly, she noticed real differences in her daily functioning:

At school:

- Could take notes without drifting off mid-lecture
- Completed assignments in class instead of running out of time
- Didn't have to reread textbook pages five times
- Raised her hand more because she could follow discussions

At home:

- Finished homework in normal amounts of time
- Could start tasks without two hours of procrastination
- Remembered to do chores without multiple reminders
- Felt less exhausted by end of day

Socially:

- Could follow conversations without losing track
- Remembered plans she'd made
- Didn't interrupt as much (could hold thoughts longer)
- Less impulsive (thought before speaking more often)

Emotionally:

- Less overwhelmed by everyday demands
- Fewer emotional meltdowns from being overstimulated
- Could regulate better when stressed
- Felt more... calm? Steady?

But Riley also noticed what *hadn't* changed:

She was still creative maybe more so, because she could actually complete creative projects instead of starting and abandoning them.

She was still funny her jokes were the same, she just timed them better.

She was still spontaneous she just also remembered to do the not-fun stuff.

She was still herself. Just... with less static between her brain and her actions.

One month in, Riley met with Dr. Chen for a follow-up.

"How's it going?" Dr. Chen asked.

Riley pulled out her journal. "It's... really good, actually. The side effects mostly went away. I can focus so much better. I'm getting my work done. I feel less overwhelmed."

"That's wonderful. And how do you feel about yourself? Your personality?"

"That's the weirdest part. I was so scared medication would change who I am. But I feel more like myself now than I did before. Like... ADHD was getting in the way of being me. Now there's less interference."

Dr. Chen smiled. "That's exactly what we hope for. The medication isn't changing you it's reducing the barriers to you being yourself."

Riley's dad, who'd come to this appointment, looked uncomfortable. "So you want to keep taking it?"

"Yeah, I do. Is that okay?"

He sighed. "I was wrong. I thought medication would make you some kind of zombie. But you're still you. Maybe even more you. If it helps, then... I support it."

Riley felt tears prick her eyes. "Thanks, Dad."

Not everything was perfect.

In February, Riley forgot to take her medication before school and felt completely scattered all day. She'd gotten used to the medication support and felt the ADHD symptoms more acutely when it wasn't there.

In March, she had a day where the medication didn't seem to work. She later realized she'd stayed up too late the night before sleep deprivation made even medication less effective.

In April, she accidentally took her medication twice (forgot she'd taken it, took it again). The double dose made her feel jittery and anxious. She called Dr. Chen, who said she'd be fine but to be more careful.

Riley learned: medication helped, but it wasn't magic. She still needed sleep, food, water, exercise, strategies, accommodations. Medication just made all of those things work better.

By the end of sophomore year, Riley had been on medication for eight months.

She'd learned what worked for her body: taking it at 7 AM with a protein breakfast, making sure to eat lunch even when not hungry, staying hydrated, getting enough sleep.

She'd learned it wasn't all-or-nothing: she could choose whether to take it on weekends depending on what she needed to do. School days, yes. Lazy Saturdays, sometimes not.

She'd learned that medication didn't solve everything: she still needed organizational systems, timers, reminders, accommodations. But those tools worked so much better when her brain could actually use them.

Most importantly, she'd learned to advocate for herself. When a teacher made a comment about "kids being overmedicated these days," Riley calmly said, "I have ADHD. Medication helps my brain function properly. It's treatment for a medical condition, not a crutch."

One day in May, Riley's friend Kayla asked, "Can I ask you about your ADHD medication?"

"Sure."

"I think I might have ADHD too. My parents are talking about evaluation. But I'm scared about medication. Does it really help? What's it like?"

Riley thought carefully. "For me, it helps a lot. But everyone's different. Some people it helps, some people it doesn't, some people don't need it at all."

"Are you glad you tried it?"

"Yeah. But it was really hard to decide. My dad was against it. I was scared. I did a ton of research. I talked to other people on medication. I made sure it was my choice, not just something a doctor told me to do."

"So how did you decide?"

"I realized the question wasn't 'Will medication change me?' The question was 'Will trying medication help me understand what support I need?' And I gave myself permission to stop if it didn't work."

"Did you ever regret it?"

Riley shook her head. "No. Because I made an informed choice. I researched, I thought about it, I tried it carefully with monitoring. Even if it hadn't worked, I wouldn't regret trying."

On the last day of school, Riley wrote a reflection for her private journal:

A year ago, I didn't know I had ADHD. Six months ago, I got diagnosed and had to decide about medication. I was so scared.

I was scared medication would change who I am.

I was scared of side effects.

I was scared of becoming dependent on a pill.

I was scared of disappointing my dad.

I was scared of making the wrong choice.

What I learned:

Medication didn't change who I am it helped me BE who I am without ADHD getting in the way.

Side effects happened but were manageable.

I'm not dependent I choose to take medication because it helps, not because I can't function without it.

My dad came around once he saw it actually helped.

There wasn't a wrong choice just a choice I made thoughtfully and can adjust if needed.

The medication isn't what makes me capable. I was always capable. The medication just reduces the interference between my capable brain and my actual performance.

Some people need medication. Some don't. Neither is better or worse. It's about what works for YOUR brain.

I'm glad I tried. I'm glad I gave myself permission to make my own choice.

I'm still me. Just with less static.

Riley closed the journal and looked at the pill bottle on her desk.

A year ago, that bottle would have terrified her.

Now it was just a tool. Like her phone alarms, her visual schedules, her accommodations, her strategies.

Just another way she'd learned to support her ADHD brain.

And she was okay with that.

———

REFLECT

Riley's story addresses one of the most personal and complicated decisions teens with ADHD face: whether to try medication. If you're facing this choice or have already made it these questions can help you process your own thoughts and feelings.

1. **Riley was caught between her dad's fear that medication would change her and her own uncertainty about what was right. Are you facing pressure from others (parents, friends, yourself) about medication?** How is that pressure affecting your ability to make your own informed choice?

   ____

   ____

   ____

   ____

2. **Riley's biggest fear was that medication would change who she was take away her creativity, humor, and spontaneity. If you're considering medication, what are your biggest fears?** Where do those fears come from (personal experience, things you've heard, concerns about dependency)?

   ____

   ____

   ____

   ____

3. **Riley discovered that medication didn't change her personality it reduced the "static" between her brain and her actions. If you're on medication, has this been**

your experience? If you're not on medication, how do you imagine it might help or not help?

———————————————

———————————————

———————————————

———————————————

4. **Riley's research showed wildly different experiences some people loved medication, others hated it, many were somewhere in between. How do you make sense of conflicting information about medication?** What sources do you trust and why?

———————————————

———————————————

———————————————

———————————————

5. **Riley learned that medication wasn't magic she still needed sleep, strategies, accommodations, and organizational systems. Do you understand that medication is one tool among many, not a cure-all?** What other supports do you have (or need) in addition to or instead of medication?

———————————————

———————————————

———————————————

———————————————

6. **Riley gave herself permission to try medication and stop if it didn't work, which made the decision less scary. If you're considering medication, does knowing you can stop if it doesn't work change how you feel**

about trying? What would make you feel safe enough to experiment?

____

____

____

____

7. **Riley noticed that her ADHD symptoms felt more obvious when she forgot her medication because she'd gotten used to functioning with support. If you're on medication, have you experienced this?** How do you feel about that dependency (is it dependency or just effective treatment)?

____

____

____

____

8. **By the end, Riley saw medication as just another tool in her ADHD management toolkit not good or bad, just useful. Whether you're on medication or not, how do you view it?** Is there shame, judgment, or acceptance around your choice?

____

____

____

____

ACT

This week, make an informed decision about ADHD medication based on education, self-assessment, and your specific needs not fear or pressure.

The ADHD medication decision is deeply personal and there's no universal right answer. Some people benefit significantly, some don't, and some manage well without it. Your task is to make YOUR choice based on informed understanding of what medication does, what you need, and what feels right for your brain and life.

Complete your "Medication Decision Framework":

Whether you're currently deciding, already on medication, or have chosen not to use it, work through this framework:

Step 1: Identify your specific ADHD challenges

List your 3 biggest ADHD struggles: (e.g., "Can't start tasks," "Forget everything immediately," "Emotional dysregulation," "Can't sit through classes")

Step 2: Research what medication addresses

Look up whether ADHD medication typically helps with YOUR specific challenges. Medication helps most with: focus, impulsivity, hyperactivity, working memory, emotional regulation. It helps less with: organization, time management (these need strategies too).

Step 3: Identify your fears and check them against facts

Write your biggest fear about medication (personality change, side effects, dependency). Then research: Is this fear based on facts or myths? Talk to your doctor about your specific concerns.

Step 4: Make YOUR decision

Not what parents want. Not what friends think. What feels right for YOUR brain based on YOUR challenges and YOUR research.

If you decide to try medication: Keep a detailed journal for 2 weeks tracking focus, side effects, mood, appetite, sleep. Use this data to evaluate whether it's helping. Remember you can stop if it doesn't work.

If you decide not to try medication: Build robust non-medication supports (accommodations, strategies, systems). Medication isn't the only path to managing ADHD successfully.

Important reminders:

- There's no "right" answer about medication only what's right for YOUR brain and situation
- Medication doesn't change your personality it helps your prefrontal cortex work more efficiently

- Taking medication isn't weakness it's treating a neurological condition, like glasses for vision
- Choosing not to take medication isn't "not trying hard enough" many people manage ADHD well without it
- You can try medication and stop if it doesn't work it's not a lifetime commitment
- Side effects are usually manageable and often improve after adjustment period
- Medication works best alongside strategies, accommodations, and systems not as sole solution
- This is YOUR decision with medical guidance others' opinions matter less than your lived experience

CHAPTER 7
STORY 7: THE ORGANIZATION MYTH

A STORY about learning that traditional organization systems don't work for ADHD brains and that you're not lazy or irresponsible, you just need different tools.

Ben Carter opened his backpack and immediately regretted it. Papers exploded outward like a magician's trick gone wrong. Crumpled homework assignments, permission slips from three weeks ago, two half-eaten granola bars, a library book that was probably overdue, and what might have been last semester's math test.

"Is that my missing soccer jersey?" his little brother Jake asked, reaching past him.

Ben grabbed it. "Maybe."

His mom appeared in the doorway, arms crossed. "Ben, we need to talk about this."

"About what?"

"About the fact that your backpack looks like a trash compactor. About the fact that your teacher emailed me again saying you didn't turn in homework. About the fact that you lost another jacket. About "

"I didn't lose the jacket. It's just... somewhere."

"Somewhere is not an acceptable answer. You're fourteen. You need to be more responsible."

Ben felt his chest tighten. He hated this conversation. They had it at least once a week.

"I'm trying," he muttered.

"Not hard enough, apparently."

After she left, Ben stared at the pile of papers on his floor. He WAS trying. He tried so hard. He'd bought three different planners this year. He'd tried color-coding his folders. He'd tried keeping everything in one binder. He'd tried the "five-minute daily cleanup" his dad suggested.

Nothing worked. Nothing ever worked.

By the third day of any system, he'd forget to use it, or lose the planner, or mix up the color codes, or shove everything in his backpack instead of filing it properly.

His brain just... didn't work the way organization systems were designed for.

Ben had ADHD. Combined type, diagnosed in sixth grade after years of teachers saying he was "smart but careless" and "needs to be more organized."

The diagnosis explained some things the constant fidgeting, the trouble focusing, the impulsivity, the homework he'd complete and then somehow never turn in.

But knowing he had ADHD didn't make him magically able to keep track of his stuff.

Freshman year was supposed to be different. New school, fresh start, better systems. Ben had promised himself he'd be organized this time.

That lasted exactly two weeks.

By late September, his locker was a disaster zone. Books stacked haphazardly, papers jammed in every crevice, gym clothes forming a questionable pile at the bottom. He'd meant to clean it out. But every time he opened the locker, the chaos was so overwhelming he'd just grab whatever he needed and slam the door shut.

His homework situation was worse. He'd complete assignments, put them in his folder, then somehow... they'd vanish. Disappeared into the black hole of his backpack, never to resurface until three weeks later when they were no longer relevant.

"Ben, where's your history homework?" Mr. Phillips asked in class.

"I did it. I swear I did it."

"Then where is it?"

Ben frantically dug through his backpack. Nothing. "I... it's here somewhere."

Mr. Phillips sighed. "That's the third time this month. I'm going to have to give you a zero."

"But I did the work!"

"If you can't turn it in, it doesn't count."

Ben wanted to scream. He'd spent two hours on that assignment. He'd understood the material. He'd written good answers. And now he was getting a zero because his backpack ate it.

Around him, other students had neat folders with organized sections. His friend Marcus had a binder with dividers and everything in the right place. His lab partner Emma could find any paper in seconds.

Why was he the only one who couldn't do this?

In October, Ben's parents instituted "organization interventions."

His dad bought him a new planner. A fancy one with sections for each class, assignment trackers, goal-setting pages.

"Write everything down," his dad said. "Every assignment, every test, every activity. Check it every morning and evening."

Ben tried. For three days, he wrote everything down diligently. By day four, he forgot the planner at home. By day six, he'd shoved it in his locker and forgotten about it. By day ten, he couldn't find the planner at all.

His mom implemented a "backpack check" system. Every night, she'd make Ben empty his entire backpack and organize it.

This worked for about a week. Then Ben started "forgetting" to do it. Not on purpose he genuinely forgot. His mom would ask if he'd done it, he'd say yes (planning to do it after dinner), then he'd get distracted by homework or his phone or literally anything, and suddenly it was bedtime and he hadn't done it.

His parents got frustrated. "Why is this so hard for you? It's simple. Just DO it."

But it wasn't simple. Ben's brain would agree to the task, fully intending to complete it, and then... the intention would just vanish. Like trying to hold water in his hands. The thought would slip away and he'd completely forget until it was too late.

November brought a new crisis: Ben lost his school laptop.

Not lost-lost. It was somewhere. But where? He'd had it Thursday. He thought he'd brought it home. But it wasn't in his room. Or his backpack. Or his locker. Or anywhere he could think of.

His parents were furious. "How do you lose a laptop?"

"I didn't mean to! I just... I can't remember where I put it."

"You need to retrace your steps."

Ben had tried. But his steps were a blur. He'd gone to class, then lunch, then more classes, then home. He must have set the laptop down somewhere. But where?

After three days of searching, he found it in the lost and found. Apparently he'd left it in the library and someone had turned it in.

"This is ridiculous," his dad said. "You're too old for this. You need to keep track of your belongings."

"I know!"

"Then why don't you?"

Because I don't know how, Ben wanted to say. Because my brain doesn't work that way. Because I can put something down and thirty seconds later have no memory of where I put it. Because I'll walk into a room with a specific purpose and immediately forget what that purpose was.

But he just said, "I'm trying."

His dad shook his head. "Try harder."

By December, Ben felt like a failure.

His grades were suffering not because he didn't understand the material, but because he kept losing assignments or forgetting to turn things in. Teachers were losing patience with his excuses. His parents were constantly frustrated. He was tired of being labeled "irresponsible" and "careless."

One afternoon, Ben's English teacher, Ms. Jackson, asked him to stay after class.

"Ben, we need to talk about your missing assignments."

"I know. I'm sorry. I just "

"I'm not mad. I'm concerned. You clearly understand the material. Your in-class work is excellent. But you're not turning in homework. What's going on?"

Ben felt tears burn behind his eyes. "I do the homework. I really do. But then I lose it. Or I forget to turn it in. Or I put it in the wrong folder. Or I don't remember I even had homework. And I've tried everything planners, folders, binders, color-coding. Nothing works. I don't know what's wrong with me."

Ms. Jackson's expression softened. "Have you talked to your counselor about this?"

"Why would I?"

"Because this sounds like it might be an executive function issue. Do you have ADHD?"

"Yeah. But what does that have to do with organization?"

"Everything. ADHD affects working memory and executive function the brain systems that help you keep track of things, remember where you put stuff, and maintain organizational systems. It's not about trying harder. It's about your brain needing different tools."

Something clicked in Ben's chest. "So I'm not just lazy?"

"Not at all. Let me set up a meeting with your counselor. I think she can help."

The following week, Ben met with Mrs. Anderson, the school counselor who specialized in students with ADHD.

"Tell me about your organizational struggles," she said.

Ben explained everything the black hole backpack, the lost assignments, the planners he'd bought and never used, the constant feeling of being behind and overwhelmed, the way his parents thought he was just irresponsible.

Mrs. Anderson listened, nodding occasionally. When he finished, she said, "Ben, you're describing classic ADHD executive function challenges. Specifically, working memory deficits and difficulty with object permanence."

"What does that mean?"

"Working memory is your brain's ability to hold and manipulate information short-term. For people with ADHD, working memory is often impaired. That's why you put your laptop down and thirty seconds later can't remember where you put it. Your brain didn't properly encode that information."

"So it's not my fault?"

"It's not about fault. It's neurology. Your brain processes and stores information about object location differently. That's why traditional organization systems don't work for you they're designed for neurotypical working memory."

"But I've tried so many systems."

"Systems designed by and for neurotypical people. We need to build systems that work for YOUR brain. Systems that work WITH your ADHD, not against it."

Mrs. Anderson taught Ben about ADHD-friendly organization principles:

Principle 1: External systems over memory

Ben couldn't rely on his brain to remember things. He needed external cues and structures.

Instead of trying to remember where things were, everything needed a specific, visible location.

Instead of trying to remember assignments, he needed external reminders.

Principle 2: Simple over complex

Complex systems required too much working memory to maintain. Ben's brain would forget the system itself.

Fewer categories. Fewer steps. Fewer things to remember.

Principle 3: Visual over written

Ben's brain responded better to visual cues than written lists or planners he had to remember to check.

If he couldn't see it, it didn't exist to his ADHD brain.

Principle 4: Digital over paper

Paper could be lost, forgotten, left in the wrong place. Digital systems lived in devices he carried everywhere.

Principle 5: Minimal maintenance

Any system requiring daily upkeep would fail. Ben needed systems that worked even when he forgot to maintain them.

"The goal," Mrs. Anderson said, "isn't to make you organized like neurotypical students. The goal is to build systems so simple and automatic that they work even with ADHD working memory challenges."

They started rebuilding Ben's organization systems from the ground up.

System 1: The Backpack Purge

Every single loose paper went into the trash. Every folder except one went home.

Ben now had: ONE folder. That's it. Everything went in the one folder. No sorting, no filing, no color-coding. Just one place.

"But won't it get messy?" Ben asked.

"Probably. But messy in one folder is better than lost in five folders.

We'll do a weekly purge every Friday, dump out the folder, throw away what you don't need."

System 2: The Digital Calendar

Goodbye planners. Ben would never check them anyway.

Instead: phone calendar with alerts. Every assignment, every test, every activity went in immediately when assigned. Three alerts per assignment: one week before, one day before, one hour before.

"Why three alerts?"

"Because your ADHD brain will dismiss the first alert. The second reminds you. The third forces you to act."

System 3: The Homework System

Ben couldn't remember to turn in homework even when he did it. New system:

As soon as homework was complete, he took a photo of it and uploaded it to the class portal immediately. No more putting it in folders to turn in later. Immediate submission.

For assignments that required physical turn-in: homework went into the front pocket of his backpack the second it was done. Nowhere else. Front pocket only.

System 4: The Daily Landing Zone

At home, everything had ONE spot:

- Backpack: hook by the door
- Phone: charging station on desk
- Laptop: desk (never moved)
- Keys: bowl by door
- Jacket: hook by door

No sorting. No thinking. Just automatic placement.

"But what if I forget?"

"That's why everything's right by the door. When you come home, you dump everything in the landing zone before you even fully enter the house. It becomes automatic."

System 5: The Sunday Reset

Once a week, Ben and his mom would spend fifteen minutes:

- Purging the ONE folder
- Checking the backpack for trash/lost items
- Reviewing the upcoming week's calendar
- Making sure homework was submitted

Not daily maintenance. Weekly. Manageable.

The first week with the new systems was weird.

Ben kept reaching for folders that didn't exist. Kept trying to remember things instead of putting them in his calendar. Kept wanting to "just set this down for a second" instead of using the landing zone.

But Mrs. Anderson had warned him: "New habits take time. Your ADHD brain likes the old way even though it doesn't work. Give it three weeks."

Week one was rough. Ben forgot to use the systems half the time.

Week two was better. The phone alerts were actually helpful. The ONE folder system meant he could find things.

Week three was when it clicked.

Ben walked in the door after school and automatically hung his backpack on the hook. Didn't think about it. Just did it.

When a teacher assigned homework, he pulled out his phone in class and added it to his calendar immediately. Three alerts set.

When he finished an essay, he uploaded it to the portal right then. Didn't wait. Didn't set it aside to submit later. Just submitted.

The systems were starting to work.

By January, Ben's life looked different.

His backpack wasn't a black hole anymore. It had one folder with that week's papers, and nothing else.

His locker was still messy, but who cared? Everything important was in his backpack.

His grades improved. Not because he was doing better work he'd always done good work but because he was actually turning things in.

His teachers noticed. "Ben, I've seen real improvement in your organization this semester. Good job."

His parents noticed too. "You haven't lost anything in three weeks. That's a record."

Ben felt something he hadn't felt in months: capable.

In February, Ben's friend Marcus asked, "How'd you get so organized? You used to lose everything."

"I didn't get organized," Ben corrected. "I built systems that work for my ADHD brain."

"What's the difference?"

"Organized people can use planners and folders and keep track of stuff in their head. I can't. So I use different tools phone calendar, one folder, digital submission. It looks different from how you organize, but it works for me."

"That's actually smart."

"Took me long enough to figure it out."

Not everything was perfect.

In March, Ben forgot to do his Sunday reset for two weeks in a row. His folder got chaotic again. He caught it before it became a disaster, but it was a reminder that his systems needed maintenance.

In April, his phone died at school and he couldn't add assignments to his calendar. He tried to remember them. Forgot two of them. Learned: carry a paper backup for emergencies.

In May, he got lazy about the landing zone and started just dropping stuff wherever. It took one lost notebook for him to recommit to the system.

Ben learned: ADHD-friendly systems still required some effort. Just less effort than traditional systems that demanded constant working memory and executive function.

On the last day of freshman year, Ben's history teacher pulled him aside.

"I wanted to tell you you've come so far this year. Beginning of the year, you were losing assignments left and right. Now you're one of the most reliable students for turning things in."

Ben felt pride swell in his chest. "Thanks. I finally figured out systems that work for my brain."

"Whatever you're doing, keep doing it."

That afternoon, Ben cleaned out his locker for summer. One folder. A few textbooks. Some random school supplies. That was it.

Last year, cleaning his locker had taken an hour of excavating papers and trash. This year took five minutes.

That summer, Ben's parents took him shopping for school supplies for sophomore year.

"Do you want some folders?" his mom asked. "Maybe a new planner?"

"Nope. One folder. That's all I need."

His dad frowned. "Are you sure? Don't you need more organization?"

"I am organized. Just differently than you think 'organized' should look."

His parents exchanged glances but didn't argue.

At home, Ben set up his landing zone for the new school year. Same hooks, same bowl, same system.

His little brother Jake watched. "Why do you do it that way?"

"Because my brain needs external structure. If I can't see where something goes, I'll forget."

"That's weird."

"That's ADHD. And it works for me."

On the night before sophomore year started, Ben reviewed his systems:
✓ One folder for all papers ✓ Phone calendar with triple alerts ✓ Digital submission for all possible assignments ✓ Landing zone by door ✓ Sunday weekly reset scheduled

Simple. Manageable. Designed for his brain, not against it.

Ben thought about the beginning of freshman year the chaos, the lost assignments, the constant feeling of failure, his parents' frustration, teachers' disappointment.

He'd spent so long thinking he was lazy or irresponsible or just bad at organization.

But he wasn't any of those things. He just had an ADHD brain that needed different tools.

Traditional organization systems were built for neurotypical working memory. They required constant mental effort to maintain. They demanded things Ben's brain simply couldn't do reliably.

But ADHD-friendly systems? Those worked WITH his brain. They were external, visual, simple, automatic. They didn't require him to remember they remembered for him.

Ben opened his phone and looked at the calendar for tomorrow. Every class period listed. Homework assignments already in there from summer work. Alerts set.

He was ready.

Not organized in the way teachers meant when they said "get organized."

But organized in the way that actually worked.

And that was what mattered.

———

REFLECT

Ben's story illustrates a fundamental truth about ADHD: traditional organization systems are designed for neurotypical working memory and executive function. If you've tried every planner, folder system, and organizational method only to have them all fail, you're not lazy or irresponsible you just need different tools.

1. **Ben described his backpack as a "black hole" where things disappeared, and he'd complete homework only to have it vanish before he could turn it in. Do you experience this?** What organizational challenges feel most frustrating or shameful for you?

____

____

____

____

2. **Ben tried multiple planners, color-coded folders, and organizational systems all designed for neurotypical brains and they all failed within days. How many organizational systems have you tried that worked briefly then fell apart?** What do those failures feel like?

____

____

____

____

3. **People kept telling Ben to "try harder" and "be more responsible," which made him feel like a failure. Have you internalized the message that you're lazy or irresponsible because traditional organization doesn't work for you?** How has that affected your self-perception?

____

____

____

____

4. **The counselor explained that Ben had working memory deficits he'd put something down and 30 seconds later couldn't remember where. Do you experience this "object permanence" challenge?** How does it impact your daily life?

____

____

____

____

5. **Ben learned that ADHD-friendly systems need to be: external (not relying on memory), simple (not complex), visual (can see it), digital (hard to lose), and low-maintenance (work even when forgotten). Which of these principles resonates most with your needs?** What makes a system work or not work for you?

____
____
____
____

6. **Ben's "one folder for everything" system seemed too simple to work, but it did because it required no sorting or decision-making. Have you avoided simple solutions because they don't look "organized enough"?** Are you trying to organize like neurotypical people instead of organizing in ways that work for your brain?

____
____
____
____

7. **Ben's parents and teachers had specific ideas about what "being organized" should look like, which didn't match what actually worked for Ben's brain. Do you face pressure to organize in traditional ways even when those ways don't work for you?** How do you advocate for systems that look different but function better?

____
____
____

---

8. **By the end, Ben stopped trying to be "organized" in the traditional sense and focused on having systems that worked, even if they looked different. What would it mean for you to stop chasing neurotypical organization and build systems designed for your ADHD brain?**

ACT

This week, stop trying to organize like neurotypical people and build ADHD-friendly systems that work for your brain.

Traditional organization systems (color-coded folders, detailed planners, complex filing systems) are designed for neurotypical working memory and executive function. Your ADHD brain needs simple, visual, external, low-maintenance systems. Your task is to drastically simplify your organizational approach and build systems so simple they work even when you forget to maintain them.

Implement the "One Place" principle for your most-lost items:

This week, choose the THREE things you lose most often (likely: backpack contents, keys, phone, assignments, etc.) and apply the ONE PLACE rule:

Example 1: School papers

OLD system: Five color-coded folders by subject (you mix them up, papers go in wrong folder, system collapses)

NEW system: ONE folder, everything goes in it, no sorting, weekly purge of old papers

Action: Buy ONE folder, label it "ALL SCHOOL STUFF," put it in backpack front pocket, use ONLY that folder

Example 2: Keys/wallet/phone

OLD system: "Put them somewhere" (you put them different places, forget where)

NEW system: ONE bowl/basket by the door, everything goes there EVERY time

Action: Put bowl by door you use most, practice depositing items there before doing anything else when you get home

Example 3: Homework tracking

OLD system: Paper planner you forget to check

NEW system: Phone calendar with THREE alerts per assignment (one week before, one day before, one hour before)

Action: Delete all paper planners, use ONLY phone calendar, set up triple-alert system

The key is: ONE place per category, VISIBLE location (can't forget what you see), SIMPLE rule (no decisions needed), LOW maintenance (works even when you forget to organize).

Important reminders:

- You're not "bad at organizing" traditional systems require working memory and executive function your ADHD brain doesn't have reliably
- Complex systems fail because they require too much mental effort to maintain simplicity is essential
- ONE folder with some mess beats five perfect folders you can't maintain
- Your organization will look different from neurotypical peers' that's okay if it WORKS
- External and visible beats hidden and sorted out of sight = out of mind for ADHD brains
- Digital systems (phone calendar, apps) are harder to lose than paper
- Weekly maintenance is more sustainable than daily maintenance
- The measure of a system is whether it functions, not whether it looks "organized"

CHAPTER 8
STORY 8: THE IMPULSE PROBLEM

A STORY about learning that impulsivity isn't about being dramatic or unpredictable it's a neurological challenge that can be managed with the right strategies and self-awareness.

Sienna Martinez raised her hand in AP Literature, but the words were already leaving her mouth before Ms. Washington could call on her.

"It's a metaphor for societal expectations crushing individual identity!"

Ms. Washington paused mid-sentence. "Sienna, I hadn't finished my question yet."

"Oh. Sorry." Sienna felt her face flush. She'd done it again. The thought had arrived in her brain with such urgency that it felt impossible not to speak it immediately.

Around her, several classmates exchanged looks. That look. The one that said: *There she goes again.*

Sienna slouched in her seat, feeling the familiar mix of embarrassment and frustration. Why couldn't she just wait? Why did every thought feel like it would evaporate if she didn't say it RIGHT NOW?

After class, her friend Maya caught up with her. "Hey, you want to come over this weekend? We're having a small thing."

"Yes! Absolutely! I'll bring " Sienna's phone buzzed. A text from her manager at the coffee shop where she'd been working for three weeks. *Can you cover a shift Saturday?*

"Actually, wait, I might have to work," Sienna said.

"Okay, let me know "

Sienna's thumbs were already flying across her phone screen: *Can't, have plans. Sorry!*

She hit send before thinking it through.

Maya's phone buzzed. She glanced at it, then at Sienna. "Did you just quit?"

Sienna looked at the text she'd sent. Oh. She'd meant to text her manager back, but she'd accidentally sent it in the group text with Maya and two other friends.

No wait she'd sent it to her manager. But she'd also written "can't have plans"? That didn't make sense.

"What did I send?" Sienna asked, confused.

Maya showed her phone. The group text read: *Quit my job lol can't deal with my manager.*

Sienna's stomach dropped. "I didn't mean to send that. I meant to " She checked her texts. She'd sent her manager: *Coming to Maya's definitely!*

"Oh my god." Sienna's hands shook as she tried to fix it. She texted her manager: *Sorry that was for someone else. I can work Saturday.*

Too late. Her manager had already responded: *If you're quitting, I need to know now.*

Sienna stared at her phone. She hadn't meant to quit. She'd just been texting too fast, not paying attention, fingers moving before her brain could supervise.

This happened all the time. Words leaving her mouth before she'd thought them through. Decisions made in seconds that should have taken careful consideration. Actions taken impulsively that she'd regret immediately afterward.

Sienna had ADHD. Hyperactive-impulsive type, diagnosed in seventh grade after years of teachers saying she "needed to think before speaking" and "made careless decisions."

The hyperactivity had mellowed somewhat as she got older. She could sit relatively still now, at least in class. But the impulsivity? That had only gotten worse.

It showed up everywhere:

In conversations: She interrupted constantly. Someone would start a sentence and Sienna's brain would anticipate where they were going, generate a response, and shove that response out of her mouth before they'd finished speaking. She didn't mean to be rude. The response just felt so urgent, like if she didn't say it immediately, it would disappear.

In decisions: She'd quit three jobs in the past year not because they were terrible, but because she'd have one bad shift and impulsively decide she was done. She'd end friendships over minor conflicts, sending dramatic texts she'd regret an hour later. She'd buy things she didn't need because the impulse to purchase felt overwhelming in the moment.

In class: She'd blurt out answers without raising her hand. She'd turn in assignments without checking them because the impulse to be DONE was stronger than the impulse to review her work.

In relationships: She'd say things she didn't mean when angry. She'd make plans and cancel them impulsively. She'd commit to things enthusiastically and then immediately regret the commitment.

People were starting to notice. Starting to pull away.

"You're so dramatic," her older sister Lucia said after Sienna's third job-quitting text in six months.

"You're unpredictable," her friend Emma said when Sienna canceled plans for the second time that month.

"You need to think before you speak," her mom said after Sienna blurted out something rude about her aunt at family dinner.

Sienna knew they were right. She knew she needed to change. But knowing and doing were completely different things.

The situation came to a head in early October.

Sienna was at a party at her friend Jordan's house. Everyone was in the backyard, talking and laughing. Sienna was having a good time maybe too good of a time. Her impulse control, never great, got even worse when she was excited or overstimulated.

Emma was telling a story about her college interview. "So the interviewer asked me about my extracurriculars, and I completely blanked "

"Oh my god, that happened to me too!" Sienna interrupted. "I was at my interview and they asked about leadership and I just "

"Sienna, I wasn't done," Emma said sharply.

"Sorry, sorry, go ahead."

Emma continued, but her tone was stiff now. Sienna felt the shift but didn't know how to fix it.

Later, Jordan mentioned he was thinking about trying out for the basketball team.

"You should totally do it!" Sienna said immediately. "I mean, you're tall, you're athletic, you'd be great "

"I don't know if I'm athletic enough," Jordan said uncertainly.

"No, you totally are! Just go for it! Don't overthink it!"

Jordan looked uncomfortable. "I was actually kind of worried about "

"You're overthinking!" Sienna said. "Just do it!"

Jordan stopped talking. The conversation moved on. Sienna didn't think much of it.

But an hour later, she overheard Emma and Maya talking in the kitchen.

"She doesn't listen," Emma was saying. "She just waits for you to stop talking so she can talk."

"I know. And she's so pushy. Jordan was trying to tell her he was nervous and she just bulldozed over his feelings."

"It's exhausting. Every conversation is just... Sienna taking over."

Sienna backed away, her chest tight. They were talking about her. They thought she was exhausting. Pushy. Not listening.

She wanted to defend herself I'm not trying to be pushy! I'm just enthusiastic! I don't mean to interrupt!

But deep down, she knew they were right.

The next day, Sienna's mom found her crying in her room.

"What's wrong, mija?"

"I'm a terrible friend. Everyone's tired of me. I can't control what comes out of my mouth."

Her mom sat on the bed. "What happened?"

Sienna explained the interrupting, the overheard conversation, the constant feeling that words left her mouth before she could stop them, the impulsive decisions that kept burning bridges.

"I don't mean to be this way. But I can't stop. It's like there's no filter between my brain and my mouth. Or between my impulses and my actions. I think something and BAM, I'm already doing it or saying it."

Her mom was quiet for a moment. "Have you talked to Dr. Reyes about this?"

Dr. Reyes was Sienna's psychiatrist who managed her ADHD medication.

"What would he say? That I need to try harder? Everyone tells me that."

"I don't think trying harder is the issue. I think this is part of your ADHD. The impulsivity. It's not about effort it's about your brain working differently."

"So I'm just stuck being like this forever?"

"No. But you need strategies. Tools. Not just 'try harder.'"

Two weeks later, Sienna sat in Dr. Reyes's office.

"Tell me about the impulsivity," he said.

Sienna explained everything the interrupting, the impulsive decisions, the words that left her mouth before she could stop them, the way she'd quit three jobs, burned friendships, made commitments she immediately regretted.

"And it's getting worse," Sienna finished. "Or maybe people are just less patient with me now that I'm seventeen. But I feel out of control."

Dr. Reyes nodded. "ADHD impulsivity is one of the most challenging symptoms because it happens so fast. The gap between impulse and action is almost nonexistent. Your brain generates a thought or urge, and before your prefrontal cortex the part that says 'wait, is this a good idea?' can weigh in, you've already acted."

"So what do I do?"

"We need to create that gap. We need to build in a pause between impulse and action. It won't be easy, and it won't be perfect. But we can slow down the process enough for you to make conscious choices instead of being driven by impulse."

Dr. Reyes taught Sienna several strategies:

Strategy 1: The Three-Second Rule

When Sienna felt the urge to speak, interrupt, or blurt something out, she needed to pause for three seconds first.

Count: One-Mississippi, Two-Mississippi, Three-Mississippi.

"Three seconds feels like forever when you have ADHD," Dr. Reyes said. "Your brain will scream at you that the thought is urgent and will disappear if you don't say it immediately. But practice holding it for three seconds. Most of the time, the thought won't disappear. And if it does? It probably wasn't as important as your impulse told you it was."

Strategy 2: The Decision Delay

For any decision bigger than "what to eat for lunch," Sienna needed to implement a mandatory waiting period:

- Small decisions (buying something, canceling plans): 10-minute wait
- Medium decisions (quitting a job, ending a friendship): 24-hour wait
- Big decisions (major life changes): One week wait

"Your impulse will tell you that you need to decide RIGHT NOW," Dr. Reyes said. "But forcing a delay lets your prefrontal cortex catch up and evaluate whether this is actually a good idea."

Strategy 3: Physical Interrupt

When Sienna felt an impulse to speak or act, she needed a physical action to interrupt the automatic response:

- Press hands together hard
- Bite tongue gently
- Squeeze something (stress ball, her own hand)
- Take a deep breath

"The physical action disrupts the impulse pathway. It gives your brain a moment to choose a response instead of reacting automatically."

Strategy 4: Scripts and Phrases

Sienna needed pre-planned phrases to use when she caught herself interrupting or being impulsive:

- "Sorry, I interrupted. Please finish your thought."
- "I'm going to think about that for a bit before deciding."
- "Can I get back to you on that?"
- "Let me write that down to remember it instead of saying it now."

Strategy 5: Medication Evaluation

Dr. Reyes wanted to evaluate whether Sienna's current ADHD medication was adequately addressing impulsivity. Sometimes medication adjustments helped with impulse control.

"Medication won't fix everything," he said. "But if your current medication isn't helping with impulsivity, we might need to adjust."

Implementing the strategies was harder than Sienna expected.

Week 1: The Three-Second Rule felt impossible.

In class, when she knew an answer, the three seconds felt like torture. Her hand would shoot up, her mouth would open, and the words would start coming out before she remembered to pause.

But she caught herself a few times. Counted to three. Let someone else answer. And the world didn't end. The thought didn't disappear.

Week 2: The Decision Delay saved her from at least two mistakes.

She got frustrated at her part-time job at the coffee shop (her fourth job this year). A customer was rude. Her manager was critical. Sienna's immediate impulse: quit.

She pulled out her phone to text "I quit" to her manager.

Then remembered: 24-hour wait for medium decisions.

She put her phone away. Took a deep breath. Finished her shift.

The next day, she felt less angry. The job wasn't perfect, but it wasn't quit-worthy. She'd been reacting to one bad shift, not to the job as a whole.

She kept the job.

Week 3: She started repairing friendships.

Sienna texted Emma: "Can we talk? I know I've been interrupting a lot and not listening. I'm working on it with my doctor. I'm sorry."

Emma responded: "Thanks for acknowledging it. Yeah, let's talk."

They met for coffee. Sienna practiced the three-second rule. Emma would say something, and Sienna would count before responding. It felt awkward and slow. But Emma seemed to relax.

"This is better," Emma said halfway through. "I can actually finish my thoughts."

"I'm trying. It's really hard. My brain wants to jump in immediately."

"I appreciate you trying."

In November, Sienna faced a real test of her new strategies.

She was at a party again Jordan's birthday this time. Everyone was there, including a guy named Tyler that Sienna had a crush on.

Tyler was talking about his plans to apply to film school. "I'm thinking about UCLA's program, but I'm not sure if my portfolio is strong enough "

Every impulse in Sienna's body wanted to interrupt: *Your portfolio is great! Just go for it! You should definitely apply!*

But she counted. One-Mississippi. Two-Mississippi. Three-Mississippi.

Tyler continued: "I guess I'm worried that my style isn't what they're looking for. I do a lot of documentary work, but I don't know if that's impressive enough."

Sienna counted again before speaking. "What kind of documentary work?"

Tyler's face lit up. "Mostly short pieces about local issues. I did one about the homeless population downtown. Another about the school funding crisis."

"That sounds really meaningful," Sienna said. She wanted to jump in with twenty more thoughts, but she paused. Let Tyler talk.

"Thanks. I just hope admissions committees think so too."

"Do you want help looking over your portfolio? I'm not an expert, but I could give you feedback."

"Actually, yeah, that would be great."

Later, Emma pulled Sienna aside. "You did really good tonight. With the listening thing."

"I'm trying. It's like... going against every instinct. My brain is screaming at me to interrupt."

"But you're doing it. That's what matters."

In December, Sienna made a decision that tested all her new strategies.

A friend asked if she wanted to go on a spring break trip a week-long trip to Mexico with five friends. The impulsive part of Sienna wanted to say YES immediately. It sounded amazing!

But she remembered: big decisions need time.

"Let me think about it and get back to you this weekend," Sienna said.

Her friend looked surprised. "You never say you'll think about things. You just decide."

"I know. I'm trying to be more thoughtful."

Over the next few days, Sienna evaluated:

- Cost: Could she afford it? She'd need to save money, work more shifts.
- Timing: Would it interfere with school? She had AP exams right after spring break.
- Relationships: Were these friends she actually wanted to spend a week with? Or was she just excited by the idea?
- Commitments: What would she have to cancel or rearrange?

After thinking it through, she decided: no. The timing was bad. She'd be stressed about exams the whole time. And honestly, two of the friends going were people she was trying to create boundaries with.

She texted her friend: "I thought about it, and I need to pass this time. Thanks for inviting me though!"

Her friend responded: "No problem! Thanks for letting me know."

Old Sienna would have said yes immediately, gotten excited, committed fully, and then either canceled last minute or gone on the trip and been miserable.

New Sienna was learning to pause. To evaluate. To make choices instead of being driven by impulses.

Not everything was perfect.

In January, Sienna had a bad day and impulsively quit her job at the coffee shop via text. Again. She'd broken her own 24-hour rule. By the time she realized her mistake, her manager had already replaced her.

"I'm disappointed," her mom said.

"I know. Me too."

"You've been doing so well with the impulse control."

"I know! But I was tired and frustrated and it just... happened. Like the old pattern kicked in before I could stop it."

Dr. Reyes wasn't surprised when Sienna told him. "Recovery isn't linear. You'll have setbacks. The question is: what did you learn?"

"That I need to be extra careful when I'm tired or stressed. That's when my impulse control is weakest."

"Exactly. So what's your plan?"

"When I'm having a bad day, I put my phone somewhere I can't reach it for at least an hour. No impulsive texts. No impulsive decisions. Forced waiting period."

"Good strategy."

By the time senior year spring semester started, Sienna had been practicing her impulse management strategies for four months.

She wasn't perfect. She still interrupted sometimes. Still made impulsive decisions occasionally. Still felt the constant urge to speak every thought immediately.

But she'd gotten better at catching herself. Better at implementing the pause. Better at asking "Is this something I actually want to do, or just an impulse?"

Her friendships had improved. Emma and Maya had both commented that conversations with Sienna felt different now more balanced, less exhausting.

Her relationship with her family had improved too. Fewer impulsive dramatic statements. Fewer decisions made in anger and regretted immediately.

And she'd kept her new job working at a bookstore for three months without quitting. When she had bad shifts, she implemented the 24-hour rule. Usually by the next day, she felt differently.

One afternoon in March, Sienna was having coffee with Tyler. They'd been hanging out regularly since she'd helped him with his film portfolio. She really liked him. A lot.

As they talked, Sienna felt the urge to say: "I like you. Like, like-you like you. Do you maybe want to go on an actual date?"

The words were RIGHT THERE. Pushing to come out. Her impulse brain was screaming: SAY IT NOW! RIGHT NOW! BEFORE THE MOMENT PASSES!

But Sienna counted. One-Mississippi. Two-Mississippi. Three-Mississippi.

She thought: Is this the right moment? Am I saying this because I genuinely want to, or because the impulse is overwhelming? How do I actually want to approach this?

She decided: not right now. She wanted to think about how to say it in a way that felt authentic, not impulsive.

The conversation continued. The moment passed. And Sienna didn't feel regretful she felt intentional.

Two days later, she texted Tyler: "Hey, I really enjoy hanging out with you. Would you want to go to dinner this weekend? Like, as a date?"

Tyler responded: "I was hoping you'd ask. Yes, definitely."

Old Sienna would have blurted it out in the coffee shop, riding the impulse. New Sienna had chosen the moment deliberately. And it felt so much better.

In May, as graduation approached, Sienna's English teacher asked the class to write a reflection on something they'd learned this year.

Sienna wrote:

This year, I learned that impulsivity isn't a personality trait it's a neurological challenge that can be managed.

For most of my life, I've been "the impulsive one." The one who quits jobs on a whim. Who interrupts constantly. Who makes decisions in seconds that should take careful thought. Who says things before thinking.

People called me dramatic, unpredictable, exhausting. And I internalized that. I thought that's just who I was.

But this year, I learned that ADHD impulsivity is neurological. My brain has almost no gap between impulse and action. The thought arrives and immediately wants to become speech or action, before my prefrontal cortex can evaluate whether it's a good idea.

Learning this didn't fix everything. But it gave me strategies:

The three-second rule. Count before speaking.

The decision delay. Wait before committing.

Physical interrupts. Pause the impulse pathway.

Scripts. What to say when I catch myself.

I'm not perfect now. I still interrupt sometimes. Still make impulsive choices. But I'm learning to create a gap between impulse and action. I'm learning to choose my responses instead of being driven by them.

I'm still enthusiastic, passionate, spontaneous those are good parts of me. But now I have more control over when and how those traits show up.

I'm not "the impulsive one" anymore. I'm someone learning to work with her ADHD brain instead of being controlled by it.

Sienna printed the essay and hung it on her wall. A reminder that change was possible. That she wasn't doomed to be ruled by impulse forever.

On graduation day, Emma hugged her. "I'm proud of you, you know."

"For graduating?"

"For growing. You've changed a lot this year."

"I'm still working on it."

"We all are. But you're actually doing the work. That's what matters."

Sienna smiled. A year ago, she would've impulsively promised to be even better, to never interrupt again, to be perfect from now on.

Now, she just said: "Thanks. That means a lot."

And she meant it.

———

REFLECT

Sienna's story addresses ADHD impulsivity one of the most socially challenging symptoms because it affects how you interact with others and make decisions. If you've been called "dramatic," "unpredictable," or "exhausting," or if you constantly regret things you've said or done impulsively, this story is for you.

1. **Sienna described having almost no gap between impulse and action thoughts would arrive and immediately become speech or action before she could evaluate them. Do you experience this?** What does the impulse-to-action pathway feel like for you?

____
____
____
____

2. **Sienna interrupted constantly, not because she was rude but because responses felt so urgent that holding them seemed impossible. Do you struggle with interrupting?** How does it feel when you're trying NOT to interrupt does the thought feel like it will disappear if you don't say it immediately?

____
____
____
____

3. **Sienna made impulsive decisions she'd regret quickly quitting jobs via text, ending friendships over minor conflicts, making commitments she'd immediately regret. What impulsive decisions have cost you?** (relationships, jobs, money, opportunities, trust?)

____
____
____
____

4. **People described Sienna as "dramatic," "unpredictable," and "exhausting," which hurt but also felt accurate. What labels have been applied to you because of impulsivity?** How have those labels affected your self-perception and relationships?

____
____

____

____

5. **Sienna's impulsivity got worse when she was excited, overstimulated, tired, or stressed. Do you notice patterns in when your impulse control is weakest?** What situations or states make impulsivity harder to manage?

____

____

____

____

6. **The three-second rule felt "like torture" to Sienna because her ADHD brain was screaming that the thought was urgent and would disappear. Have you tried pausing before speaking or acting?** What makes pausing so difficult?

____

____

____

____

7. **Sienna learned to distinguish between enthusiasm/spontaneity (good traits) and impulsivity that damages relationships or creates regret. Can you identify which of your impulsive behaviors are harmful and which are actually positive expressions of your personality?** Where's the line for you?

____

____

____

____

8. **By the end, Sienna wasn't "cured" but had tools to create a gap between impulse and action. If you could slow down your impulse-to-action pathway even slightly, what would change in your life?** What relationships, decisions, or situations would improve?

____

____

____

____

ACT

This week, create a 3-second gap between impulse and action.

ADHD impulsivity means almost no pause between urge and action thoughts become words or behaviors before your prefrontal cortex can evaluate whether they're good ideas. The pain is real, but the rejection often isn't. Your task is to build that crucial gap so you can choose your responses instead of being driven by impulses.

Practice "The Three-Second Rule" in conversations this week:

Every time you feel the urge to speak, interrupt, or blurt something out, COUNT before speaking:

- One-Mississippi
- Two-Mississippi
- Three-Mississippi

Your ADHD brain will SCREAM that:

- The thought is urgent and will disappear
- The moment will pass
- You'll forget what you wanted to say
- Someone else will say your idea

But here's what actually happens when you wait three seconds: The thought usually DOESN'T disappear. And if it does? It probably wasn't as important as your impulse brain told you it was.

Practice this 10 times this week. Start with low-stakes conversations (family dinner, casual friend chats). Notice:

- Does the thought actually disappear? (Usually no)
- Does waiting improve the interaction? (Usually yes people feel more heard)
- Can you hold the thought for three seconds? (Gets easier with practice)

For bigger impulses (quitting job, canceling plans, sending dramatic texts), add a mandatory waiting period:

- Small decisions: 10-minute wait
- Medium decisions (quitting, ending friendships): 24-hour wait
- Big decisions: One week wait

Set a timer. During the wait, you can't act on the impulse. After the wait, you can choose and you'll often find the impulse has passed or you see it differently.

Important reminders:

- Impulsivity is neurological your brain has almost no gap between impulse and action by default
- You're not "dramatic" or "unpredictable" you have ADHD impulsivity that needs management strategies
- The three-second pause feels like torture at first that's the ADHD urgency signal lying to you
- Thoughts usually DON'T disappear if you wait that's the biggest impulsivity lie
- Physical interrupts help (press hands together, bite tongue gently) to disrupt the impulse pathway
- You'll still make impulsive mistakes while learning focus on quick repair, not perfection
- Impulsivity gets worse when tired, stressed, or overstimulated plan for high-risk times

- Some impulsivity is positive (spontaneity, courage, enthusiasm) you're not trying to eliminate it, just manage it

CHAPTER 9
STORY 9: THE RESTLESS MIND

STORY 9: **The Restless Mind**

A story about learning that your body's need for movement isn't misbehavior it's how your nervous system regulates, and accommodating that need is self-care, not weakness.

Chris Walker sat in fourth period AP Biology, his leg bouncing so fast it was making his entire desk vibrate. He pressed his foot flat against the floor, trying to stop it. The bouncing stopped for exactly three seconds before starting again, seemingly of its own accord.

His lab partner, Hannah, glanced at his leg, then back to her notes. She didn't say anything, but Chris saw her subtly shift her chair away from the vibrations.

Ms. Lopez was explaining cellular respiration. Chris was trying to listen he actually found biology interesting but his body was screaming at him. Move. Stand. Walk. Pace. Anything but sit still for one more second.

He'd been sitting for thirty-five minutes. Five more minutes until the bell. It felt impossible.

Chris tapped his pencil against his notebook. Silently at first, then with increasing intensity.

"Chris," Ms. Lopez said, not unkindly. "The pencil."

"Sorry." He set the pencil down. Ten seconds later, he was tapping his foot again.

By the time the bell rang, Chris practically exploded out of his seat. He needed to move. Needed to walk, run, pace, anything.

His friend Marcus caught up with him in the hallway. "Dude, you okay? You looked like you were going to jump out the window."

"I hate sitting still. It's like torture."

"It's just school, man. Everyone has to sit."

"Yeah, but for you it's just boring. For me it's physically painful."

Marcus gave him a skeptical look. "Painful? Come on."

Chris wanted to explain the way his muscles tensed, the way energy built up inside him with nowhere to go, the way sitting still made him feel like he was crawling out of his skin. But how could he make someone understand who didn't feel it?

Chris had ADHD. Hyperactive type, diagnosed in third grade when his teacher said he "couldn't sit still for five minutes" and was "constantly disrupting class with his movement."

The diagnosis helped explain why Chris had always been this way: bouncing in his seat, fidgeting with everything, unable to stay seated during story time, running instead of walking, climbing on things, moving, moving, always moving.

His parents had tried everything when he was younger: removing sugar from his diet, more exercise, sports to "burn off energy," consequences for getting out of his seat, rewards for sitting still, occupational therapy.

Some things helped a little. Sports gave him an outlet. Occupational therapy taught him some regulation strategies. But nothing eliminated the fundamental problem: Chris's body needed to move. Not wanted to move needed to move. Like breathing. Like eating. Essential.

And high school, with its seven-period day of sitting in hard plastic chairs for fifty minutes at a time, felt like prison.

Sophomore year started rough.

In English, Chris's teacher, Mr. Rodriguez, had a strict "no movement" policy. Students had to sit in their assigned seats, face forward, no fidgeting with anything that made noise or distracted others.

The first week, Mr. Rodriguez called Chris out three times for bouncing his leg, tapping his pencil, and leaning his chair back on two legs.

"Chris, we've talked about this. You need to sit properly and stay still."

"I'm trying."

"Try harder."

By week two, Mr. Rodriguez sent Chris to the office for "repeated disruption."

The vice principal, Mrs. Anderson, looked at Chris with tired patience. "This is the third time you've been sent here for movement issues. What's going on?"

"I can't help it. I have ADHD. I need to move."

"Everyone has to sit still in class. That's part of being a student."

"But "

"No buts. You're fifteen. You're old enough to control yourself. Figure it out."

Chris went back to class feeling defeated. Control himself. Like his body's need for movement was a discipline problem he just wasn't trying hard enough to fix.

In October, things escalated.

Chris's geometry teacher, Mr. Santos, was explaining proofs at the board. Chris had been sitting for forty minutes. His whole body was restless. He started bouncing his leg. Then tapping his fingers. Then shifting in his seat. Then leaning back in his chair.

"Chris, four legs on the floor."

Chris complied. Two minutes later, he was bouncing his knee again.

"Chris, the leg."

He stopped. One minute later, he was tapping his pencil.

"Chris!"

"I'm sorry! I can't "

"You can and you will. If I have to tell you one more time, you're getting a detention."

Chris tried. He really tried. He pressed both feet flat on the floor. Put his hands in his lap. Sat up straight.

The restlessness built. And built. And built.

It felt like his skin was too small for his body. Like his muscles were vibrating. Like if he didn't move immediately, he would explode.

Without thinking, Chris stood up.

"Chris! Sit down!"

"I just need to "

"Sit. Down. Now."

Chris sat. But standing for those three seconds had felt like finally breathing after holding your breath underwater.

Mr. Santos sent him to the office with a detention slip.

That night, Chris's parents had "the talk" with him.

"We got an email from Mr. Santos," his mom said. "This is getting out of hand."

"I know. I'm trying."

"You need to try harder," his dad said. "You're too old for this. You need to learn to sit still like everyone else."

"I can't! I physically can't!"

"That's an excuse."

"It's not!" Chris felt tears of frustration burning his eyes. "You think I want to get in trouble? You think I like disrupting class? I hate it! But sitting still feels impossible. Like actually impossible."

His mom's expression softened. "Honey, other kids with ADHD manage to sit in class."

"Do they? Or do they just hide it better? Or maybe their ADHD is different than mine?"

His parents exchanged looks.

"What do you want us to do?" his dad asked.

"I don't know! But telling me to try harder doesn't work. I've been trying harder my entire life."

The next week, Chris's mom made an appointment with his doctor, Dr. Kim.

"Tell me what's happening," Dr. Kim said.

Chris explained the constant restlessness, the physical need to move, the way sitting felt painful, the teachers who thought he was being disruptive on purpose, the detentions, the frustration, the feeling of being trapped in his own body.

"How many hours a day are you expected to sit still at school?" Dr. Kim asked.

"Like... six? Seven? Not counting lunch."

"And how long can you comfortably sit without movement?"

Chris thought. "Maybe twenty minutes? Thirty if I'm really interested in what's happening?"

Dr. Kim nodded. "Chris, your hyperactive ADHD means your nervous system requires movement to regulate. It's not behavioral it's neurological. Asking you to sit still for six hours is like asking someone to hold their breath for six hours."

"So I'm not just being difficult?"

"Not at all. Your body is telling you it needs movement. That's a real, physical need."

"But my teachers don't believe that."

"Then we need to advocate for accommodations. You shouldn't have to suffer through school because your body works differently."

Dr. Kim wrote a letter for the school outlining Chris's needs:

Chris has ADHD, predominantly hyperactive type. His nervous system requires frequent movement to regulate and maintain focus. Requiring him to sit completely still for extended periods is counterproductive and causes significant distress.

Recommended accommodations:

- *Permission to stand at his desk or move to the back of the room when needed*
- *Access to fidget tools (stress balls, fidget spinners, therapy putty)*
- *Scheduled movement breaks (5 minutes every 30-45 minutes)*
- *Seating near the door for easy, non-disruptive exits*
- *Permission to pace while working independently*
- *Alternative seating options (standing desk, wobble stool, exercise ball)*

Chris's mom met with the school counselor and his teachers to implement these accommodations.

Not all teachers were receptive.

Mr. Rodriguez: "I don't think it's fair to other students if Chris gets to stand and move around while they have to sit."

The counselor: "The Americans with Disabilities Act requires reasonable accommodations. Movement breaks aren't an advantage they're leveling the playing field."

Mr. Santos: "Won't this be disruptive to other students?"

The counselor: "If Chris can move to the back of the room or step into the hallway, it's actually less disruptive than him fidgeting constantly at his desk."

Eventually, reluctantly, all his teachers agreed to try the accommodations.

The first day with accommodations felt weird.

In English, Chris had a fidget spinner in his pocket. Mr. Rodriguez had moved his seat to the back corner. When Chris felt restlessness building, he pulled out the fidget spinner.

It helped. Not completely he still needed to bounce his leg but having something in his hands reduced the overall restlessness level from 9 to about 6.

In geometry, Mr. Santos had placed a standing desk option at the back of the room. When Chris felt like he couldn't sit anymore, he raised his hand. "Can I stand?"

Mr. Santos hesitated, then nodded.

Chris moved to the standing desk. Immediately, the trapped feeling eased. He could shift his weight. Bounce slightly. Stretch. And he could still see the board, still take notes, still participate.

By the end of the period, he realized: he'd learned more standing than he usually did sitting. Because he wasn't spending all his mental energy trying to force his body to be still.

Not everyone was supportive.

Some classmates made comments: "Must be nice to get special treatment." "Why does he get to stand and we don't?" "That's so distracting."

Chris tried to ignore it. But one day in the cafeteria, a guy from his English class said loudly, "Hey Chris, why don't you just learn some self-control?"

Chris's friend Marcus jumped in before Chris could respond. "He has ADHD, man. His brain works different. Lay off."

"ADHD is just an excuse for lazy people who can't behave."

Chris felt anger flash through him. "You want to trade? You want to feel what it's like to sit in class feeling like you're going to crawl out of your skin every single day? You want to be told you're disrupting class just by existing in your own body? You want to be called lazy and undisciplined when you're trying so hard it hurts?"

The guy backed off. "Whatever, man."

But the interaction stuck with Chris. People thought accommodations were special treatment. They didn't understand that accommodations didn't give him an advantage they just removed a barrier.

Over the next few months, Chris figured out what worked for him:

Fidget tools: He found that a smooth stone in his pocket worked better than fidget spinners. Silent, discreet, grounding.

Movement breaks: He learned to recognize when he hit his limit (about 30-35 minutes) and would ask to step into the hallway for a quick walk. Two minutes moving, then back to class.

Strategic scheduling: He talked to his counselor about scheduling his hardest classes (ones requiring most sitting) earlier in the day when he had more capacity to manage restlessness. By sixth period, his tolerance was lowest.

Physical outlets: He joined the track team. Running after school helped discharge some of the built-up restless energy. On days with track practice, he found sitting in class slightly easier.

Standing/alternative seating: He worked out with his teachers which classes could accommodate standing desks. Not all could, but having it in two or three classes made a huge difference.

Stigma management: He stopped being embarrassed about his needs. When students asked why he got to stand, he said simply: "I have ADHD and my body needs movement to function. It's a medical accommodation."

In January, something unexpected happened.

A freshman named Mateo approached Chris after school. "Hey, uh, I heard you have ADHD?"

"Yeah."

"And you get to stand in class and stuff?"

"Yeah, why?"

"I think I have ADHD too. Like, I can't sit still either. It drives my teachers crazy. But I didn't know you could get accommodations for it."

Chris felt something shift. "You should talk to your counselor. Get evaluated if you haven't been. You don't have to suffer through sitting all day."

"But like... isn't it embarrassing? Everyone staring at you when you stand up?"

"Sometimes. But you know what's more embarrassing? Getting detention every week for something you can't control. Or failing classes because you're using all your energy trying to sit still instead of learning."

Mateo nodded slowly. "Thanks, man."

A week later, Chris saw Mateo standing at the back of one of his classes, fidgeting with something in his hands.

Chris smiled. One more person who didn't have to feel trapped.

In March, Chris had a revelation during biology.

Ms. Lopez was teaching a particularly complex unit on genetics. Chris was standing at his designated standing desk in the back, shifting his weight, bouncing slightly, fidgeting with his stone.

He realized: he was absorbing everything. He understood the concepts. He was engaged.

When he sat, his brain was divided: 60% trying to force his body to be still, 40% trying to learn. When he stood and could move freely, 100% of his brain was available for learning.

The movement wasn't a distraction from learning. It was what enabled learning.

After class, he approached Ms. Lopez. "Can I ask you something? When I'm standing in the back, is it distracting to other students?"

Ms. Lopez smiled. "Honestly? I barely notice anymore. And your grades have improved since you started using the standing desk. You're more engaged, asking better questions."

"So it's helping?"

"Clearly. You're not the same student who could barely make it through class in September."

By spring, Chris had made peace with his restless body.

He'd spent so many years thinking something was wrong with him. That he just needed more discipline. That if he tried hard enough, he could force his body to be still like everyone else.

But now he understood: his body's need for movement was like someone needing glasses to see. Not a moral failing. Not a discipline problem. A neurological difference that needed support, not suppression.

One afternoon in May, Chris's dad picked him up from track practice.

"How was practice?"

"Good. I'm getting faster."

They drove in silence for a moment. Then his dad said, "I owe you an apology."

Chris looked at him, surprised.

"I thought you could just... control it. The movement thing. I thought it was a behavior you could change if you tried hard enough. I didn't understand it was physical. Neurological."

"It's okay, Dad."

"It's not. I made you feel like you were failing at something you couldn't control. I'm sorry."

Chris felt his throat tighten. "Thanks."

"I'm proud of you, you know. For advocating for yourself. For figuring out what you need. That takes courage."

On the last day of school, Mr. Rodriguez asked Chris to stay after class.

Chris braced himself. Even with accommodations, Mr. Rodriguez had been the most skeptical teacher all year.

"I wanted to tell you," Mr. Rodriguez said, "that I was wrong."

"About what?"

"About you. At the beginning of the year, I thought you were being disruptive on purpose. I thought accommodations were coddling you. But I've watched you this year. You work harder than most students in that class. You're not trying to get out of work you're trying to access the learning despite a real barrier. I'm sorry I didn't see that sooner."

Chris didn't know what to say.

"Keep advocating for yourself," Mr. Rodriguez continued. "The world isn't designed for people whose bodies need to move. But that doesn't mean you should have to suffer. It means the world needs to adapt."

That summer, Chris volunteered at a camp for kids with ADHD.

Many of the kids had the hyperactive type like him. They couldn't sit through activities. They were constantly in motion. Their counselors were getting frustrated.

Chris talked to the camp director. "Why are we making them sit? Why not design activities that involve movement?"

They redesigned the schedule: nature hikes while learning about ecosystems, science experiments done while walking around outdoor stations, storytelling where kids acted out the story instead of sitting and listening, math games that involved running and jumping.

The kids thrived. They were engaged. They were learning. Because the activities worked with their bodies instead of against them.

One little kid, maybe eight years old, said to Chris: "This is the first camp where I don't get in trouble for moving."

Chris felt that deeply. "Yeah. Me too."

The night before junior year started, Chris prepared his backpack.

Inside: fidget stone, water bottle, running shoes for track practice, planner, notebooks.

He'd advocated for his accommodations to continue next year. Standing desk access in key classes. Movement breaks. Fidgets. Seating by the door.

He wasn't nervous like he'd been before sophomore year. Because he knew now: his body's need for movement wasn't something to fight or suppress. It was something to accommodate and work with.

Chris wrote in his journal that night:

For fourteen years, I thought something was wrong with me. I thought I just needed more discipline, more control, more willpower.

But my body's need to move isn't a character flaw. It's neurology. It's how my nervous system regulates.

Sitting still for hours isn't a moral virtue. It's just one way of existing. Not the only way. Not the best way for everyone.

I'm not disrupting class by moving. I'm accessing education despite a world designed for bodies that don't need what mine needs.

Accommodations aren't special treatment. They're equity. They remove barriers.

My restless body isn't a problem to solve. It's a reality to accommodate.

And I'm done apologizing for existing in a body that moves.

Chris closed the journal and looked at himself in the mirror.

Sophomore year Chris had felt broken, wrong, constantly in trouble for something he couldn't control.

Junior year Chris understood: he wasn't broken. The system was broken.

And he'd learned to build his own supports within that broken system.

That would have to be enough.

REFLECT

Chris's story addresses the physical restlessness of hyperactive ADHD the body's neurological need for movement that's often misunderstood as misbehavior or lack of discipline. If you've been told to "just sit still," "stop fidgeting," or "control yourself," this story is for you.

1. **Chris described sitting still as "physically painful" and like "crawling out of his skin," but people didn't believe him because they couldn't feel it. Do you experience this physical need for movement?** How would you describe what restlessness feels like in your body?

   ____

   ____

   ____

   ____

2. **Chris could sit comfortably for about 20-30 minutes before the restlessness became unbearable. What's your**

limit? How long can you sit before you feel that urgent need to move?

____

____

____

____

3. **People kept telling Chris to "try harder" and "control yourself" as if his movement was a discipline problem. Have you internalized the message that your need for movement is misbehavior or lack of self-control?** How has that affected your self-perception?

____

____

____

____

4. **Chris realized he was using 60% of his brain trying to force his body to be still and only 40% actually learning. When you're forced to suppress movement, how much of your mental energy goes to sitting still versus to learning/working?** What could you accomplish if you didn't have to fight your body?

____

____

____

____

5. **Chris discovered that when he could move freely (standing, fidgeting, pacing), he actually learned better 100% of his brain was available instead of divided. Have you noticed that movement actually helps you**

focus rather than distracts you? How does your learning/work change when you're allowed to move?

____

____

____

____

6. **Chris faced judgment from classmates who saw his accommodations as "special treatment." How do you navigate the visibility of needing to move when others don't understand it's a neurological need, not a privilege?** What would help others understand?

____

____

____

____

7. **Chris learned that accommodations (standing desks, fidgets, movement breaks) weren't giving him an advantage they were removing a barrier. Do you have access to movement accommodations?** If not, what holds you back from requesting them?

____

____

____

____

8. **By the end, Chris understood that his restless body wasn't a problem to solve but a reality to accommodate. What would it mean for you to stop fighting your body's need for movement and start building systems that work with it?**

____

____

____

____

ACT

This week, accommodate your body's need for movement instead of suppressing it.

ADHD hyperactivity means your nervous system requires movement to regulate not wants to move, NEEDS to move, like breathing. Forcing yourself to sit still for extended periods isn't discipline; it's fighting your neurology. Your task is to build movement into your day intentionally instead of battling your body.

Identify your sitting tolerance and build movement breaks around it:

For three days, track: How long can you actually sit before restlessness becomes urgent? (Be honest not how long you "should" sit, but how long you can sit before feeling like you'll explode)

Most people with hyperactive ADHD can sit comfortably for 20-30 minutes before needing movement. If that's you, your schedule needs movement breaks every 20-30 minutes not every hour (which is when neurotypical people need breaks).

This week, implement one of these movement accommodations:

Option 1: Scheduled movement breaks

Set phone timer for your sitting tolerance (20-30 min). When timer goes off, take a 2-minute movement break: walk, stretch, do jumping jacks, pace. Then return to work. Repeat all day.

Option 2: Standing while working

Do homework at a standing desk or tall counter. You can shift weight, bounce slightly, stretch while working. Track: Do you focus better standing than sitting?

Option 3: Discrete fidgets

Keep a smooth stone, therapy putty, or fidget cube in your pocket. Use it constantly during class/meetings. The hand movement reduces overall restlessness.

Option 4: Request accommodations

If you don't have formal accommodations, talk to your counselor about: permission to stand during class, access to standing desk, movement breaks, seating near door for easy exits. These are legitimate medical accommodations covered by disability law.

Important reminders:

- Your body's need for movement is neurological, not behavioral it's not a discipline problem
- Sitting tolerance limits are real stop trying to meet neurotypical standards your body can't sustain
- Movement accommodations are medical support, not special treatment they level the playing field
- Fidgeting and movement help ADHD brains focus they're not distractions from learning
- You don't need to apologize for existing in a body that moves
- Accommodations aren't training wheels they're permanent supports you'll always need
- Daily intense exercise helps increase sitting tolerance (but doesn't eliminate need for movement breaks)
- The world is designed for bodies that can sit still that's a design flaw, not your personal failing

CHAPTER 10
STORY 10: THE PRIORITY PUZZLE

A STORY about learning that ADHD doesn't just make it hard to prioritize it makes everything feel equally urgent or equally irrelevant, and you need external frameworks to create hierarchy where your brain sees none.

Maya Chen stared at her to-do list, paralyzed.

She had twelve things to accomplish today. Twelve tasks of wildly varying importance. But looking at the list, every single item felt exactly the same. Equally urgent. Equally important. Equally impossible.

1. Finish college essay (due in 3 days)
2. Organize desk drawer
3. Study for chemistry quiz (tomorrow)
4. Text Aunt Linda back (from 2 weeks ago)
5. Research volunteer opportunities for college apps
6. Clean bathroom
7. Start math homework (due Friday)
8. Call about dentist appointment
9. Read 2 chapters for English (due next week)
10. Update college application spreadsheet
11. Reply to college emails
12. Find missing library book

Maya knew, logically, that finishing her college essay was more important than organizing her desk drawer. That studying for tomorrow's chemistry quiz should come before reading for next week's English class. That calling about a dentist appointment was less urgent than texting her aunt back.

But her brain didn't know that. To her ADHD brain, all twelve items existed in the same flat plane. No hierarchy. No priority. Just an overwhelming list of THINGS that all screamed for attention simultaneously.

So Maya did what she always did when everything felt equally important: she picked the easiest, most immediately satisfying task.

She organized her desk drawer.

Three hours later, the drawer was perfectly organized. Color-coded pens. Labeled sections. Everything in its place.

And her college essay was still blank. The chemistry quiz was tomorrow morning. She'd accomplished nothing that actually mattered.

Maya had ADHD. Inattentive type, diagnosed in ninth grade after years of being called "smart but disorganized" and "not working up to her potential."

The ADHD explained a lot: the difficulty focusing, the zoning out in class, the executive function challenges, the way time seemed to either crawl or disappear completely.

But what it explained most was the prioritization problem.

For neurotypical people, tasks seemed to naturally arrange themselves into hierarchies. Important versus unimportant. Urgent versus non-urgent. Big versus small. Their brains could look at a list and instinctively know what to tackle first.

Maya's brain couldn't do that. Every task existed in the same undifferentiated mass. She'd spend two hours perfecting a minor assignment worth 10 points, then have no time left for a major project worth 100 points. She'd deep-clean her entire room when she had a test the next day. She'd research random topics that interested her while college applications sat untouched.

It wasn't that she didn't care about important things. It's that her brain couldn't distinguish important from unimportant. Without external hierarchy, everything was the same.

Junior year was when the prioritization problem became critical.

College applications. SAT prep. AP classes. Extracurriculars for her college resume. Volunteer work. Part-time job. Social life. Family obligations. Self-care.

Too many demands. Too many decisions. Too many things that all felt equally pressing and equally ignorable.

In September, Maya's college counselor, Mrs. Harper, called her in for a meeting.

"Maya, we need to talk about your college application timeline."

Maya pulled out her planner. Or tried to. Where was her planner? She'd had it this morning. Or was that yesterday?

She found a crumpled piece of paper with dates written on it. That would work.

Mrs. Harper handed her a printed timeline. "Here are the important deadlines. Early Action is November first. Regular Decision is January first. You need to have your Common App essay done by October, so you have time to revise."

Maya looked at the timeline. It was color-coded, organized, clear.

It meant nothing to her brain.

"Okay," she said.

"Maya, I need you to prioritize this. College applications are the most important thing you'll do this fall."

"I know."

"Do you? Because I haven't seen you at any of our essay writing workshops. You haven't submitted your activities list. You haven't requested letters of recommendation yet."

"I'll do it this weekend."

Mrs. Harper gave her a look that said she'd heard that before. "You need a system. A way to prioritize. Because right now, you're letting urgent-but-unimportant things crowd out important-but-not-urgent things."

Maya nodded, not entirely sure what that meant.

That weekend, Maya sat at her desk, determined to work on her college essay.

She opened her laptop. Stared at the blank document.

Her phone buzzed. A text from her friend Olivia about weekend plans. Maya spent twenty minutes responding, planning, coordinating.

She returned to the essay. Blank page. What was the prompt again? She opened the Common App website to check. While there, she started browsing college websites. Went down a rabbit hole researching dorm life at various schools. An hour disappeared.

She snapped back to attention. The essay. Right.

But now she noticed her desk was messy. How could she write with all this clutter? She spent thirty minutes organizing papers, throwing things away, creating piles.

She returned to the laptop. Cursor blinking. Mocking her.

She decided she needed a snack first. In the kitchen, she got distracted helping her younger brother with his homework. That took forty-five minutes.

By the time she returned to her room, it was dinner time.

After dinner, she was exhausted. She'd been "working" on the essay for six hours. She'd written exactly zero words.

In October, the pressure mounted.

Maya had a chemistry test on Friday. A major English paper due Monday. Her college essay still unfinished. SAT prep. A shift at her part-time job at the library. A family dinner on Sunday she'd promised to help cook for.

On Tuesday, she made a list of everything she needed to do.

She stared at the list. Which thing first?

She decided to work on the English paper. But first she needed to read the book. She'd read most of it, but not the last three chapters. She started reading.

Two hours later, she'd read one chapter and fallen down a Wikipedia rabbit hole about the author's life.

Wednesday: Chemistry test was in two days. She should study. But the English paper was also looming. And she really needed to make progress on the college essay. And she'd promised to help her brother with his science project. And her boss had texted asking if she could pick up an extra shift.

Maya felt panic rising. Too many things. All equally demanding. No way to know which to prioritize.

So she did laundry instead. Laundry had clear steps. Clear completion. Unlike the amorphous pile of responsibilities that all screamed "DO ME FIRST."

Thursday night, Maya had a complete breakdown.

The chemistry test was tomorrow. She'd barely studied. The English paper was due Monday and she hadn't started. The college essay deadline was approaching and she still had nothing. She'd agreed to an extra work shift on Saturday that she now regretted. Her room was a disaster despite spending hours on laundry.

She sat at her desk, crying, surrounded by papers and responsibilities and decisions she couldn't make.

Her mom found her like that. "Maya, what's wrong?"

"Everything. I don't know what to do first. I have too many things and they all feel equally important and I can't figure out which one to prioritize so I just end up doing nothing or doing the wrong thing and now I'm failing everything."

Her mom sat down. "Let's make a list. We'll figure it out together."

"I have a list! Lists don't help! I look at the list and every item feels the same!"

Her mom was quiet for a moment. "Have you talked to your therapist about this?"

Maya saw a therapist, Dr. Martinez, who specialized in ADHD.

"Not really."

"I think you should. This seems like more than just time management. This seems like you need help with prioritization."

The next week, Maya met with Dr. Martinez.

"Tell me about the prioritization challenge," Dr. Martinez said.

Maya explained everything the lists that didn't help, the way every task felt equally urgent or equally irrelevant, the hours spent on small things while major deadlines loomed, the paralysis when faced with multiple demands, the inability to figure out what to do first.

"It's like my brain can't see hierarchy," Maya said. "Other people look at a list and just know what's most important. I look at a list and it's just... flat. Everything on the same level."

Dr. Martinez nodded. "That's executive function deficit. Your brain struggles with prioritization because ADHD affects the ability to evaluate importance, urgency, and consequence. You're not being irresponsible. Your brain literally processes all tasks as equivalent unless you build external structure to create hierarchy."

"So what do I do?"

"We're going to build external prioritization frameworks. Tools that do the work your brain can't do automatically."

Dr. Martinez taught Maya several prioritization systems:

System 1: The Eisenhower Matrix

Divide all tasks into four categories:

1. **Urgent AND Important:** Do first (Chemistry test tomorrow, college essay due soon)
2. **Important but NOT Urgent:** Schedule time for these (Reading for next week, SAT prep)
3. **Urgent but NOT Important:** Delegate or minimize (Some texts, minor requests)
4. **Neither Urgent NOR Important:** Eliminate or do last (Organizing desk, random research)

"Your ADHD brain sees everything in category 1 or category 4," Dr. Martinez explained. "Either EVERYTHING is urgent, or nothing matters. This framework forces you to evaluate each task across two dimensions: urgency and importance."

System 2: The Point System

Assign point values based on actual consequences:

- Major test tomorrow: 10 points
- College application deadline: 10 points
- Minor homework assignment: 2 points
- Text to friend: 1 point
- Organizing desk: 0 points

"Your brain won't naturally create this hierarchy," Dr. Martinez said. "But you can assign points based on actual consequences: What happens if this doesn't get done? Grade impact? Deadline? Long-term importance?"

System 3: The One-Thing Rule

When overwhelmed, don't try to prioritize everything. Ask: "If I could only accomplish ONE thing today, what would have the biggest positive impact?"

Do that thing first. Everything else is secondary.

System 4: Deadline Proximity + Impact

Multiply urgency (how soon) by importance (how much it matters):

- Due tomorrow, worth 100 points = High priority
- Due next week, worth 50 points = Medium priority
- Due in a month, worth 10 points = Low priority
- No deadline, worth anything = Lowest priority

System 5: External Accountability

Work with someone who CAN prioritize naturally (parent, coach, counselor) to help rank your tasks. Your brain might not see hierarchy, but theirs can.

Maya started implementing the systems, beginning with the Eisenhower Matrix.

She wrote out all her current tasks and forced herself to categorize them:

URGENT & IMPORTANT:

- Finish college essay draft (due in 5 days)
- Study for chemistry test (tomorrow)
- Complete English paper outline (due Monday)

IMPORTANT but NOT URGENT:

- Schedule SAT retake
- Request letters of recommendation
- Start reading next book for English

URGENT but NOT IMPORTANT:

- Reply to non-critical texts
- Attend club meeting she didn't care about

NEITHER URGENT NOR IMPORTANT:

- Organize desk
- Research random colleges she wasn't applying to
- Deep-clean room

Looking at the matrix, priorities became clear in a way they'd never been before. Her brain saw: "Okay, focus on the upper-left quadrant. Everything else can wait."

She started with the chemistry test studying. Set a timer for two hours. When the timer went off, she moved to the college essay. Worked for ninety minutes. Then the English paper outline.

It wasn't perfect. She still got distracted. Still felt the pull of easier, less important tasks. But having the external framework helped. When she felt herself drifting toward organizing her desk, she could look at the matrix and see: that's literally in the "neither urgent nor important" category. It doesn't deserve my time right now.

Over the next month, Maya refined her approach.

She worked with her mom every Sunday to prioritize the week ahead. Her mom, who didn't have ADHD, could look at Maya's task list and immediately identify what mattered most.

"College essay," her mom said definitively. "That's your top priority until it's done."

"But I also have "

"I know. But if you could only work on one thing this week, it should be that essay. Everything else comes after."

The One-Thing Rule. Maya wrote "COLLEGE ESSAY" on a sticky note and put it on her laptop. Every time she got distracted or paralyzed by choices, the note reminded her: this is the priority.

She also started using the point system for daily tasks. Each morning, she'd assign points to everything on her list:

- Chemistry homework: 5 points (due tomorrow, affects grade)
- College essay: 10 points (major deadline, huge impact)
- Text friend back: 1 point (nice to do, not critical)

- Organize notes: 0 points (no real consequence if not done)

Then she'd work down the list from highest to lowest points. When she felt paralyzed about what to do next, she'd look at the numbers. The numbers didn't lie. Her brain might feel like texting her friend was urgent, but the points said: do the 10-point task first.

In November, Maya's college counselor noticed the change.

"Maya, I got your essay draft. This is excellent work."

"Thanks. I'm trying to prioritize better."

"I can tell. You've also submitted your activities list, gotten your recommendation letters, and you're ahead of many students. What changed?"

"I learned that my ADHD brain can't prioritize naturally. So I have to use external systems. Matrices, point values, working with my mom. If I don't build hierarchy externally, my brain just sees everything as the same."

Mrs. Harper smiled. "That's impressive self-awareness. Keep it up."

Not everything was smooth.

In December, Maya had a particularly overwhelming week. Finals approaching. College applications due. Two major projects. Holiday obligations. Part-time job.

She tried to use her systems, but there were too many high-priority items. Everything was urgent AND important. The matrix didn't help when everything belonged in the upper-left quadrant.

She called Dr. Martinez. "What do I do when everything is actually high priority?"

"Then you need to add another layer of evaluation. Among the urgent and important tasks, which one has the earliest deadline? That's first. Then the next earliest. Then the next. Break ties using consequences: which one affects your future most if it fails?"

Maya created a new system: Priority Within Priority.

All her urgent-and-important tasks got sub-ranked:

1. College app essay (due in 2 days) = Priority 1
2. Chemistry final (in 3 days) = Priority 2
3. English project (due in 5 days) = Priority 3

She worked through them sequentially. No multitasking. No switching. One at a time, highest to lowest.

It worked. Not perfectly she was still stressed and exhausted. But she got everything done. Not because she somehow gained the ability to naturally prioritize, but because she'd built external scaffolding her brain could follow.

In January, Maya submitted her last college application.

She looked at the timeline Mrs. Harper had given her in September. Somehow, impossibly, she'd met every deadline.

Not because it had been easy. Not because her brain had magically learned to prioritize. But because she'd learned to work with her brain's limitations.

She thought about September Maya, paralyzed by her to-do list, spending hours organizing a desk drawer while major deadlines loomed.

That Maya had thought the problem was laziness. Or poor time management. Or lack of discipline.

But the real problem was neurological. Her ADHD brain couldn't create hierarchy. Couldn't distinguish important from unimportant, urgent from non-urgent. Everything existed in an undifferentiated mass of TASKS.

Learning prioritization systems hadn't fixed her brain. But it had given her tools to work around the deficit.

In February, Maya's friend Jasmine asked for help.

"I don't understand how you got all your college apps done. I'm drowning. I have so much to do and I don't know where to start."

"Do you have ADHD?" Maya asked.

"Yeah. Why?"

"Because ADHD brains can't naturally prioritize. We need external frameworks."

Maya taught Jasmine the Eisenhower Matrix. Showed her the point system. Explained the One-Thing Rule.

"This is actually really helpful," Jasmine said, filling in her matrix. "Looking at this, I can see what matters and what doesn't. Before, it all felt the same."

"That's exactly what I felt. Like everything was equally important or equally irrelevant."

"So you just... use these systems all the time?"

"Pretty much. If I don't, I default to doing easy-but-unimportant things and avoiding hard-but-important things. The systems override my brain's default."

By spring semester, Maya had integrated prioritization frameworks into her daily life.

Every Sunday: Week planning session with her mom. Identify the One Thing for the week. Rank all tasks using the matrix.

Every morning: Assign point values to that day's tasks. Work highest to lowest.

When paralyzed: Ask "If I could only do one thing right now, what would matter most?" Do that thing.

When everything felt important: Use deadline proximity to break ties. Earliest deadline wins.

She wasn't perfect. She still got distracted sometimes. Still spent too long on minor tasks occasionally. Still felt the pull of organizing or researching random topics when she should be working on important things.

But she was functional in a way she'd never been before.

One afternoon in April, Maya was working on a scholarship application. It was due in a week. It was important could be worth $5,000.

Her phone buzzed. A friend asking if she wanted to hang out.

Old Maya would have immediately said yes, prioritizing the immediate social request over the future-oriented scholarship.

New Maya looked at her matrix. The scholarship was in the "important but not urgent yet" quadrant. Hanging out was "neither urgent nor important."

But hanging out was more appealing. More immediately rewarding.

Maya thought: If I could only do one thing today that would have the biggest positive impact on my future, what would it be?

The scholarship application.

She texted back: *Can't today, working on scholarship app. Want to hang out this weekend?*

Her friend responded: *Sure! Good luck with the app.*

Maya returned to the application. It wasn't that she'd suddenly gained willpower or discipline. It was that the external framework had given her clarity her brain couldn't generate alone.

On the last day of junior year, Maya cleaned out her locker.

She found old to-do lists from the beginning of the year. Flat, undifferentiated lists where every item existed on the same plane. No wonder she'd been paralyzed.

She looked at her current to-do list. Each item had a point value. Each was categorized by urgency and importance. The hierarchy was external, visible, clear.

Her brain still couldn't naturally prioritize. But it didn't have to. She had systems that did it for her.

That summer, Maya worked as a camp counselor. She used her prioritization systems to manage counselor responsibilities:

- Urgent & Important: Camper safety, immediate behavioral issues
- Important not Urgent: Lesson planning, building relationships with campers

- Urgent not Important: Minor camper requests that could wait
- Neither: Perfectionist tendencies to make everything "just right"

The other counselors noticed. "You're so organized. How do you keep track of everything?"

Maya almost laughed. Organized? Her brain was chaos. But she'd built external structure to contain the chaos.

"I have ADHD," she explained. "My brain can't naturally prioritize, so I use frameworks to create hierarchy externally. Want me to teach you?"

Several counselors said yes. Turned out, even people without ADHD found the systems helpful.

The night before senior year started, Maya prepared for the year ahead.

She'd been accepted to her first-choice college. Full scholarship. She'd accomplished things that had seemed impossible back in September of junior year.

Not because she'd fixed her brain. But because she'd learned to work with it.

She created her first weekly matrix for senior year. Filled in the quadrants. Assigned point values. Identified her One Thing for the week.

Her younger sister watched. "That looks like a lot of work."

"It is. But you know what's more work? Being paralyzed by a list of tasks and not knowing where to start. Spending hours on things that don't matter while important deadlines loom. Feeling like you're constantly failing because you can't figure out what to prioritize."

"Is that what it's like? With ADHD?"

"For me, yeah. Everything feels equally important or equally irrelevant. My brain just doesn't create hierarchy naturally. So I have to build it externally."

Her sister looked at the matrix with new understanding. "That makes sense."

Maya wrote in her journal that night:

For years, I thought I was just bad at time management. That if I tried harder, I could figure out what to prioritize.

But ADHD doesn't just make it hard to manage time. It makes it impossible to naturally see hierarchy. Important versus unimportant. Urgent versus non-urgent. Big versus small.

My brain sees: TASKS. Undifferentiated. Overwhelming. Paralyzing.

Learning prioritization systems didn't fix my brain. But it gave me external frameworks to create the hierarchy my brain can't generate alone.

The Eisenhower Matrix. The point system. The One-Thing Rule. Deadline proximity.

These tools do the work my executive function can't do automatically.

I'm not lazy. I'm not irresponsible. My brain just needs external scaffolding to function in a world designed for brains that naturally prioritize.

And now I have that scaffolding.

Maya closed the journal and looked at her organized desk not because she'd spent three hours avoiding important work, but because she'd scheduled fifteen minutes for it after completing high-priority tasks.

Prioritization didn't come naturally to her brain.

But with the right systems, it didn't have to.

———

REFLECT

Maya's story addresses one of the most frustrating ADHD executive function challenges: the inability to naturally prioritize. If you've ever stared at a to-do list feeling completely paralyzed because everything feels equally important (or equally irrelevant), this story is for you.

1. **Maya described looking at her to-do list and seeing all tasks as "exactly the same equally urgent, equally important, equally impossible." Do you experience this**

flat, undifferentiated view of tasks? What does it feel like when you can't figure out what to do first?

____

____

____

____

2. **Maya would spend hours on small, easy tasks (organizing a desk drawer) while major deadlines loomed (college essay). Do you find yourself gravitating toward easy-but-unimportant tasks instead of hard-but-important ones?** What tasks do you use to avoid the things that actually matter?

____

____

____

____

3. **Maya's therapist explained that her ADHD brain couldn't evaluate importance, urgency, and consequence everything existed on the same flat plane. Does this match your experience?** When you look at a to-do list, can you instinctively know what's most important, or does it all blur together?

____

____

____

____

4. **Maya felt paralyzed when faced with multiple demands, unable to figure out which to tackle first, so she'd often end up doing nothing. Does decision**

paralysis happen when you have too many options? What does that paralysis feel like?

____

____

____

____

5. **Maya learned she needed external frameworks (matrices, point systems, working with someone who could prioritize) because her brain couldn't create hierarchy naturally. Have you tried prioritization systems?** What's worked and what hasn't?

____

____

____

____

6. **When everything was actually urgent and important, Maya needed "priority within priority" sub-ranking based on earliest deadline. Do you face situations where multiple things genuinely are high-priority simultaneously?** How do you break those ties?

____

____

____

____

7. **Maya's mom could look at her task list and immediately identify what mattered most because her neurotypical brain could see hierarchy. Do you have someone in your life who can help you prioritize when you can't?** How does it feel to need that external perspective?

---

8. By the end, Maya still couldn't naturally prioritize, but she had systems that did it for her. What would it mean for you to stop trying to develop natural prioritization skills and instead build external frameworks that work for your brain?

ACT

This week, use the Eisenhower Matrix to create external priority hierarchy your brain can't generate alone.

ADHD executive function deficits mean your brain can't naturally evaluate importance, urgency, and consequence everything feels equally important or equally irrelevant. Your task is to build external frameworks that create the priority hierarchy your brain can't create automatically.

Use the Eisenhower Matrix to categorize every task this week:

Write down EVERYTHING you need to do (school, home, work, social, personal). Then force each item into one of four categories:

QUADRANT 1: Urgent AND Important

Action: DO FIRST

Examples: Test tomorrow, major deadline this week, crisis situations

Rule: Work ONLY on Quadrant 1 until it's empty

QUADRANT 2: Important but NOT Urgent

Action: SCHEDULE specific time for these

Examples: Long-term projects, SAT prep, exercise, relationship building

Rule: Put these in your calendar with specific time blocks or they'll never get done

QUADRANT 3: Urgent but NOT Important

Action: MINIMIZE time here

Examples: Some texts/emails, minor requests from others, interruptions

Rule: These feel urgent but don't actually matter do them fast or skip them

QUADRANT 4: Neither Urgent NOR Important

Action: ELIMINATE or do last (if ever)

Examples: Organizing for the sake of organizing, random research, perfectionist tendencies

Rule: Your ADHD brain goes here when avoiding Quadrants 1 and 2 resist this

When you feel paralyzed about what to do next, look at your matrix. The answer is visible: Do Quadrant 1 items first. Always.

Important reminders:

- You don't naturally see hierarchy your ADHD brain sees tasks as flat/undifferentiated without external structure
- Feelings about urgency often lie trust the framework, not your emotions about what feels pressing
- Easy tasks feel more urgent than hard tasks but easy ≠ important
- Working with someone who CAN prioritize naturally (parent, counselor) helps you build your matrix accurately
- You'll need external prioritization frameworks permanently this isn't training until you "learn" to prioritize naturally
- When multiple things are in Quadrant 1, use earliest deadline to break ties
- The "One Thing Rule": If you could only do ONE thing today, what would have biggest impact? Do that first.
- Prioritization systems aren't weakness they're accommodation for executive function deficit

CHAPTER 11

STORY 11: THE MEMORY GAP

A STORY about learning that forgetting isn't carelessness it's working memory deficit, and you need external systems to remember what your brain can't hold.

Isaiah Brooks stood in the doorway of his bedroom, completely blank on why he'd come upstairs.

He'd been in the kitchen. His mom had asked him to do something. Something upstairs. What was it?

He retraced his steps mentally. Kitchen. Mom talking. He'd been getting a snack. She'd said... something.

Nothing. The memory was just gone.

He walked back downstairs. "Mom, what did you ask me to do?"

His mom sighed. "Isaiah, I literally just told you thirty seconds ago. Get your phone charger from your room."

"Right. Sorry."

He went back upstairs. Walked into his room. Stood there.

Wait. Phone charger. Right. Where was it?

He checked his desk. Not there. His nightstand. Not there. Under his bed. Not wait, why was he looking under his bed?

Oh right. Phone charger.

Twenty minutes later, he found it tangled in his sheets. By the time he brought it downstairs, his mom had already borrowed his sister's charger.

"Never mind," she said. "I got one."

Isaiah felt the familiar flush of frustration and shame. He wasn't trying to be difficult. He'd genuinely forgotten. Multiple times. In the span of twenty minutes.

Isaiah had ADHD. Combined type, diagnosed in sixth grade after years of teachers saying he was "bright but forgetful" and "doesn't follow directions."

But it wasn't just forgetting. It was working memory the brain's ability to hold information actively in mind while using it.

For neurotypical people, working memory was like a mental whiteboard. They could hold a teacher's multi-step instructions, remember what they were doing while doing it, keep track of several things simultaneously.

Isaiah's working memory was more like an Etch A Sketch. Information appeared briefly, then one shake one distraction, one new thought and it was gone.

Senior year started, and Isaiah's working memory challenges became impossible to ignore.

In AP Calculus, Mr. Johnson explained a multi-step problem at the board. "First, you'll factor the polynomial. Then take the derivative.

Then set it equal to zero and solve for x. Then plug back into the original equation to find the y-coordinate."

Isaiah wrote furiously: Factor. Derivative. Set to zero. Solve. Plug back.

But by the time he started working the problem, he'd already forgotten step two. Was it take the derivative first, or set it equal to zero first? He looked at his notes. They just said "derivative" with no context.

He raised his hand. "Can you repeat the steps?"

Mr. Johnson looked slightly annoyed. "I just explained this. Were you not paying attention?"

"I was. I just... forgot."

"You need to listen more carefully."

But Isaiah had been listening. He'd been listening so hard his brain hurt. The information just didn't stay. It was like trying to hold water in his hands the harder he gripped, the faster it slipped through his fingers.

In October, Isaiah's forgetfulness escalated.

His mom asked him to stop at the store on the way home from school for three things: milk, bread, and eggs.

Isaiah repeated them in his head the entire drive. Milk, bread, eggs. Milk, bread, eggs. Milk, bread, eggs.

He got to the store. Grabbed milk. Walked to the bread aisle. What was the third thing? He stood there, trying to remember. Milk, bread, and... something.

He texted his mom: "What was the third thing?"

She responded immediately: "Eggs. I told you five minutes ago."

He got the eggs. At checkout, he realized he'd forgotten the bread. He'd been so focused on remembering eggs that bread had vanished from his working memory completely.

At home, his mom was frustrated. "Isaiah, this is getting ridiculous. You can't remember three items for five minutes?"

"I tried! I repeated them the whole way!"

"You need to write things down."

"I was driving. I couldn't write."

"Then use your phone voice memo. Or tell Siri to remind you. You need to stop relying on your memory. It clearly doesn't work."

The words stung because they were true. His memory didn't work. At least, not the part of memory that held things actively in mind.

November brought the real crisis.

Isaiah had a major history project due. Mr. Chen had explained the requirements in class: "You'll need a thesis statement, five primary sources, three secondary sources, proper citations in MLA format, and a works cited page. Ten pages minimum. Due November 30th."

Isaiah wrote down: Thesis, 5 primary, 3 secondary, MLA, works cited, 10 pages, Nov 30.

When he sat down to work on the project two weeks later, he looked at his notes. They made no sense. What was a primary source again? Was the thesis supposed to be one page or was that part of the ten pages? Was MLA the one with parentheses or footnotes?

He couldn't remember. The details Mr. Chen had explained the specific examples, the clarifications, the context were completely gone.

He spent two hours Googling "what is a primary source" and "how to do MLA format" and "how long should a thesis statement be." Information he'd been told in class. Information that had entered his brain and then immediately evaporated.

By the time he finally started writing, he was so exhausted from trying to reconstruct the instructions that he could barely focus on the actual content.

The worst incident happened in mid-November.

Isaiah was taking his SAT. The proctor gave instructions: "When I say begin, open your test booklet to section 1. You'll have 65 minutes for this section. Fill in your answers on the answer sheet, not in the test booklet. If you finish early, you may review your work but do not move ahead to the next section."

Isaiah thought he understood. When the proctor said "begin," he opened the booklet and started working.

Ten minutes in, he realized he'd been filling in answers in the test booklet instead of the answer sheet.

Panic flooded through him. He'd have to transfer all his answers. That would take time. Time he didn't have.

He raised his hand. "I made a mistake. Can I "

"No talking during the test. Figure it out."

Isaiah spent the next five minutes frantically transferring answers, erasing work from the booklet, filling in bubbles. By the time he finished transferring, he'd lost fifteen minutes and completely disrupted his concentration.

His scores came back two weeks later. Lower than his practice tests by 150 points.

His college counselor was disappointed. "Isaiah, you're capable of better scores. What happened?"

"I forgot to use the answer sheet. I filled everything in the wrong place and had to transfer it all."

"You need to pay more attention to instructions."

Isaiah wanted to scream. He HAD paid attention. He'd listened to every word. He'd repeated the instructions to himself. And somewhere between hearing "use the answer sheet" and actually taking the test, that information had vanished from his brain.

That night, Isaiah had a breakdown in front of his parents.

"I can't keep doing this. I can't remember anything. I listen to instructions and they disappear. I write things down and forget what my notes mean. I repeat things to myself and still forget. I'm trying so hard and my brain just... doesn't work."

His dad, who also had ADHD, understood in a way his mom didn't. "You have working memory deficits. I have them too. It's not about trying harder. It's about building external systems."

"What does that even mean?"

"It means you can't rely on your brain to hold information. You need external memory tools that remember for you."

The next week, Isaiah's dad took him to see Dr. Park, his psychiatrist.

"Tell me about the memory issues," Dr. Park said.

Isaiah explained everything forgetting instructions thirty seconds after hearing them, losing track mid-task, forgetting what he'd come into rooms for, the multi-step directions that evaporated immediately, the SAT disaster.

"What you're describing is classic ADHD working memory deficit," Dr. Park said. "Your brain has limited capacity to hold information actively in mind. Think of working memory like RAM in a computer it's temporary storage space for what you're currently working on. People with ADHD have significantly less RAM than neurotypical people."

"So I'm just... stuck with this?"

"You can't increase your brain's RAM. But you can build external memory systems so you don't have to rely on working memory alone."

Dr. Park outlined strategies:

Strategy 1: Write everything down immediately

Not later. Not "I'll remember to write this down." The second you receive information, write it. Phone notes, paper, whatever. Bypass working memory entirely.

Strategy 2: Voice memos for anything verbal

Teacher giving instructions? Voice memo. Parent asking for three things from the store? Voice memo. Can't write it down fast enough? Record it.

Strategy 3: Photos for visual information

Board notes, written instructions, where you parked your car, where you set something down take a photo immediately.

Strategy 4: Checklists for multi-step tasks

Break everything into steps. External checklist eliminates need to remember what comes next.

Strategy 5: Alarms and reminders

Set them the moment you think of something. "I'll remember later" is a lie your brain tells you.

Strategy 6: Immediate action when possible

If you can do it right now (respond to email, put something away, complete a task), do it. Don't rely on remembering to do it later.

Isaiah started implementing the systems, beginning with voice memos.

In calculus, when Mr. Johnson explained a multi-step problem, Isaiah held his phone under his desk and recorded the explanation. Later, he could listen back as many times as needed.

At home, when his mom asked him to do something, he immediately opened his phone and set a reminder. No more relying on his brain to remember for the five minutes it took to finish his current task.

When he parked at the mall, he took a photo of where he'd parked. No more twenty-minute searches through parking lots trying to remember where he'd left the car.

For his history project, he took photos of the assignment instructions on the board. When he needed to reference them later, they were right there no trying to decipher incomplete notes.

The systems helped, but Isaiah still struggled.

In December, he had an important college interview. The interviewer asked, "Tell me about a time you overcame a challenge."

Isaiah started talking about his debate competition. Midway through the story, he completely lost track of where he was going with it. He'd started with a specific point he wanted to make, but the point had evaporated from his working memory mid-sentence.

He fumbled, tried to recover, ended up rambling. The interviewer looked confused.

After the interview, Isaiah sat in his car, frustrated. He'd prepared. He'd practiced. But in the moment, his working memory had failed him again.

He called his dad. "I messed up the interview. I lost track of what I was saying mid-answer."

"Did you practice your stories out loud?"

"I practiced in my head."

"That's not enough for working memory deficits. You need to write out your stories, practice speaking them aloud multiple times, maybe even record yourself. Rehearsal builds procedural memory, which is more reliable than working memory."

Isaiah spent the next week preparing for his second interview differently. He wrote out answers to common questions. Practiced them aloud ten times each. Recorded himself and listened back. The repetition moved the information from fragile working memory to more stable long-term memory.

The second interview went much better. He still lost track once or twice, but he'd rehearsed enough that he could recover.

In January, Isaiah's history teacher pulled him aside.

"Isaiah, I noticed you've been taking photos of the board and using voice memos. I wanted to check do you have accommodations?"

Isaiah felt defensive. "I'm not cheating. I'm just "

"I'm not accusing you of cheating. I'm asking if you have formal accommodations, because if not, you should."

"Oh. I have ADHD. Working memory problems. I can't remember multi-step instructions."

"You should talk to your counselor about getting a 504 plan. Accommodations might include: copies of notes/instructions, recorded lectures, extended time for tests, ability to use notes on tests with multi-step problems."

Isaiah had never thought about formal accommodations. He'd been suffering through, assuming everyone struggled the same way.

The following week, he met with his counselor. With Dr. Park's documentation, they created a 504 plan:

- Copies of all written instructions and notes
- Permission to audio record lectures
- Access to teacher notes/study guides
- Extended time on tests (working memory makes processing slower)
- Ability to use reference sheets for multi-step procedures

The accommodations made a massive difference.

In calculus, Mr. Johnson now gave Isaiah a written step-by-step guide for complex problems. Isaiah could refer to it instead of trying to hold all the steps in his head simultaneously.

In English, when the teacher gave essay instructions, Isaiah received a written handout with all the requirements. No more frantically scribbling notes that made no sense later.

In lab science, Isaiah could photograph the procedure steps. No more forgetting what he was supposed to do next halfway through the experiment.

By February, Isaiah had built a comprehensive external memory system:

For school:

- Photograph all board notes and instructions
- Audio record lectures (with permission)
- Written step-by-step guides for procedures
- Checklists for multi-step assignments
- Calendar with all deadlines and details

For home:

- Voice memos for any verbal requests
- Reminders set immediately when thinking of something
- Notes app for everything (shopping lists, tasks, ideas)
- Photos of where he put things
- Leaving items in visible places (can't forget what he sees)

For conversations:

- Taking notes during important talks
- Asking people to text him important information
- Repeating back what he heard to confirm
- Writing down appointments/plans immediately

The systems worked. Not perfectly he still forgot things sometimes. But the catastrophic memory failures became rare instead of constant.

In March, Isaiah's friend Lucas asked, "How do you remember everything? You're always prepared."

Isaiah almost laughed. "I don't remember anything. That's why I'm prepared."

"What?"

"I have ADHD. My working memory is terrible. So I photograph everything, record everything, write everything down, set reminders for everything. I don't rely on my brain to remember. I rely on external systems."

"That seems like a lot of work."

"You know what's more work? Forgetting things constantly, having to ask people to repeat themselves, losing track mid-task, redoing work because you forgot the instructions."

Lucas nodded slowly. "I actually forget a lot of stuff too. Think I could use some of your systems?"

"Sure. It's really just: don't trust your brain. Externalize everything."

In April, Isaiah was studying for AP exams. The sheer volume of information to remember felt overwhelming.

But Isaiah had learned: he didn't need to remember it all. He needed to organize it externally so he could access it.

He created study guides with step-by-step procedures. Flashcard apps for memorization. Voice memos of himself explaining concepts. Photos of important charts and diagrams. Reference sheets with formulas.

During the exams, he couldn't use most of these tools. But the process of externalizing the information helped him learn it more deeply. And for math and science exams where formula sheets were allowed, having his own organized reference sheet was invaluable.

His scores came back in July: 5 on Calculus, 4 on History, 4 on English. Good scores. Better than he'd expected.

Not because he had a great memory. Because he'd learned to work around his terrible one.

The summer before college, Isaiah's dad sat him down.

"College is going to be harder. Bigger lectures, more independence, more responsibility for remembering things. You need to make sure you have your systems in place."

"I know."

"And you need to advocate for yourself from day one. Register with disability services. Get accommodations set up before classes start. Don't wait until you're struggling."

Isaiah nodded. His dad was right. He couldn't hide his working memory deficits anymore. He needed to be upfront about what he needed.

In August, Isaiah arrived at college orientation. During the disability services session, he registered and explained his ADHD and working memory challenges.

"We can provide note-taking services, recorded lectures, extended time, access to professor notes whatever you need," the coordinator said.

Isaiah felt relief. He wouldn't have to fight for accommodations. They were built into the system.

His first day of classes, he introduced himself to each professor after class.

"Hi, I'm Isaiah. I'm registered with disability services for ADHD. I have working memory deficits, so I'll be audio recording lectures and may need to reference written instructions for assignments. I wanted to let you know up front."

Most professors were supportive. "No problem. I'll make sure to provide written instructions for everything."

One professor was skeptical. "You'll need to learn to remember things without accommodations eventually."

Isaiah stood his ground. "Actually, I won't. I have a documented disability that affects working memory. I'll always need external systems. Just like someone with poor vision will always need glasses. Accommodations aren't training wheels. They're permanent supports."

The professor backed down. "Fair enough."

Two months into college, Isaiah ran into his roommate frantically searching their dorm room.

"What are you looking for?"

"My student ID. I put it down somewhere and now I can't find it."

Isaiah pulled out his phone and showed his roommate his "Where is it?" photo album. "I take a photo every time I put something important down. Wallet, keys, ID, phone charger. Then I don't have to remember where things are."

His roommate stared. "That's genius. I lose stuff all the time."

"You probably have better working memory than me. But the system works for anyone."

Over the semester, Isaiah noticed several of his floor-mates adopting his strategies. Voice memos for assignments. Photos of whiteboard notes. Reminders set immediately. External systems that removed the burden of remembering.

Turned out, even people with decent working memory appreciated tools that reduced mental load.

At Thanksgiving break, Isaiah's mom commented, "You seem more organized this semester."

"I'm not more organized. I just have better systems."

"What's the difference?"

"Organization implies I'm good at keeping track of things mentally. I'm not. But I've built external scaffolding that does the remembering for me. My brain hasn't changed. My tools have."

His younger sister, a high school sophomore, asked, "How do you remember to use all those systems?"

"Most of them are automatic now. When I hear instructions, my hand goes to my phone for voice memo. When I set something down, I take a photo. When I think of something I need to do, I set a reminder. It's habit."

"But doesn't that take a lot of effort?"

"Less effort than forgetting things constantly and dealing with the consequences."

Isaiah made it through his first semester of college with a 3.6 GPA. Not perfect, but solid.

More importantly, he'd made it through without the catastrophic memory failures that had plagued him in high school.

He'd forgotten things, sure. But with external systems in place, the forgetting was caught early. He'd check his phone notes and see what he'd missed. He'd listen to voice memos and remember what had been said. He'd look at photos and see what he needed.

His brain still couldn't hold much in working memory. But it didn't have to. Technology remembered for him.

One night in December, Isaiah wrote in his journal:

For seventeen years, I thought I was just careless. That if I paid better attention or tried harder, I'd remember things.

But ADHD working memory deficits aren't about attention or effort. They're about capacity. My brain's RAM is limited. Information comes in, and if I don't immediately externalize it, it vanishes.

I used to think relying on external systems was cheating or weakness. Like I should be able to remember things "naturally" like everyone else.

But now I understand: accommodating my working memory limits isn't weakness. It's adaptation. It's working with my brain instead of against it.

I'll never have typical working memory. That's a neurological reality.

But I can build systems so comprehensive that it doesn't matter.

Isaiah closed the journal and looked at his phone full of notes, voice memos, photos, reminders, alarms, lists, and external memory of every kind.

His brain couldn't hold it all.

But his systems could.

And that was enough.

———

REFLECT

Isaiah's story addresses ADHD working memory deficits the brain's limited ability to hold information actively in mind. If you've been told you're "not paying attention" or "being careless" when you genuinely can't remember things you just heard, this story is for you.

1. **Isaiah would forget instructions thirty seconds after hearing them, forget why he'd walked into a room, and lose track of what he was doing mid-task. Do you experience this immediate forgetting?** What does it feel like when information just vanishes from your mind?

____

____

____

____

2. **Isaiah described working memory as "like trying to hold water in your hands the harder you gripped, the faster it slipped through your fingers." Does this capture your experience?** How would you describe what working memory challenges feel like?

____

____

____

____

3. **People kept telling Isaiah to "pay more attention" or "listen more carefully" when he WAS paying attention the information just didn't stay. Have you been blamed for memory failures that aren't about attention or effort?** How has that affected your self-perception?

____

____

____

____

4. **Isaiah wrote down notes but then couldn't remember what they meant or what context they had. Do you struggle with incomplete notes or forgetting the context of information you wrote down?** How does this impact your ability to study or follow through on tasks?

____
____
____
____

5. **Isaiah's dad explained that he needed "external memory systems" because he couldn't rely on his brain to hold information. Does knowing that working memory deficits are neurological (not about trying harder) change how you view your forgetting?**

____
____
____
____

6. **Isaiah discovered that voice memos, photos, and immediate note-taking bypassed his working memory entirely information went straight to external storage. Have you tried externalizing information immediately instead of trying to remember it?** What's worked and what hasn't?

____
____
____
____

7. **Isaiah needed formal accommodations (recorded lectures, written instructions, extended time) to succeed academically. Do you have access to working memory accommodations?** If not, what holds you back from requesting them?

____

____

____

____

8. **By the end, Isaiah understood he'd never have typical working memory, but he could build systems so comprehensive it didn't matter. What would it mean for you to stop trying to "fix" your memory and instead build external systems that work for your brain?**

____

____

____

____

ACT

This week, stop relying on your working memory and externalize information immediately.

ADHD working memory deficits mean your brain has extremely limited capacity to hold information actively in mind like a computer with very little RAM. Information enters and immediately evaporates unless you externalize it. Your task is to bypass your working memory entirely by creating external memory systems.

Implement "The Second You Hear It" rule for all information:

This week, practice immediate externalization for every piece of information you receive. Never tell yourself "I'll write it down later" or "I'll remember that" both are lies your working memory tells you.

Your immediate externalization toolkit:

For verbal instructions/assignments:

Teacher explaining project → Open phone notes and type it immediately, OR start phone recording

Parent asking you to do something → Set phone reminder with details right then

Friend making plans → Text yourself or put in calendar the second they say it

For visual information:

Board notes → Take photo before leaving class

Written instructions → Photograph them

Where you parked → Photo of location/sign

Where you put important items → Photo of the spot

For your own thoughts:

"I should remember to..." → Reminder set NOW, not later

"Don't forget to..." → Goes in task list immediately

"I need to..." → Alarm/calendar entry right then

Practice this 20 times this week. Every single time information enters your brain, immediately externalize it. No middle step of "holding it in memory" straight from hearing/seeing to external storage.

Also, request formal working memory accommodations if you don't have them: recorded lectures, copies of notes, written instructions, extended time on tests. Working memory deficits qualify for these supports.

Important reminders:

- Working memory deficits are neurological you CAN pay attention and still not remember
- "I'll remember it later" is the biggest lie working memory tells externalize IMMEDIATELY or it's gone
- Your working memory capacity is limited and won't increase you need permanent external systems
- Multi-step instructions are nearly impossible without external support that's neurology, not personal failing
- Photos, voice memos, and notes aren't crutches they're legitimate accommodations for real deficits

- Forgetting isn't carelessness it's insufficient RAM in your brain
- Accommodations (recorded lectures, written instructions, extended time) are your legal right
- The goal isn't to improve your working memory it's to bypass it entirely through external tools

CHAPTER 12
STORY 12: THE ADHD ADVANTAGE

A STORY about learning that ADHD isn't just a collection of deficits it comes with genuine strengths that, when recognized and cultivated, can become your greatest assets.

Ava Rodriguez stared at the college essay prompt on her screen: *Describe a challenge you've faced and how you've grown from it.*

She knew exactly what challenge to write about. ADHD. The diagnosis that had defined her high school experience. The explanation for why everything was so much harder for her than for everyone else.

But every time she started writing, the essay became a list of everything ADHD made difficult:

I struggle to focus. I get distracted easily. I have trouble organizing my thoughts. I forget things constantly. I'm impulsive. I interrupt people. I can't manage time well. I lose things. I procrastinate. I...

Ava deleted the paragraph for the third time. This essay was supposed to show growth and resilience. But all she could write about was what ADHD took from her. What it prevented her from doing. How it made everything harder.

She couldn't think of a single positive thing ADHD had given her. Not one strength. Not one advantage. Just an endless list of ways her brain didn't work right.

Ava had ADHD. Combined type, diagnosed freshman year after years of teachers saying she was "smart but unfocused" and "capable of more." The diagnosis had been a relief finally, an explanation for why she struggled. But it had also become her identity in a way she wasn't sure was healthy.

She was "the girl with ADHD." The one who needed accommodations. The one who forgot assignments. The one whose brain worked differently. The one who couldn't do things the "normal" way.

And now, applying to colleges, she was supposed to write about herself. Her strengths. Her potential. Her future.

But when she thought about herself, all she saw was ADHD. And when she thought about ADHD, all she saw were problems.

In October, Ava met with her college counselor, Ms. Kim.

"How's the essay coming?" Ms. Kim asked.

"It's not. I'm writing about my ADHD, but every time I try, it just becomes this depressing list of everything I struggle with."

"What do you struggle with?"

Ava rattled off the list: focus, organization, time management, impulsivity, forgetfulness, procrastination.

Ms. Kim listened, then asked, "What are you good at?"

Ava blinked. "What?"

"What are your strengths?"

"I... I don't know. I'm okay at art? I like writing when I can actually focus. I'm good at coming up with ideas."

"Tell me more about that."

"About what?"

"Coming up with ideas. Give me an example."

Ava thought. "Like... in English class, when we have to analyze a text, I always see connections other people don't. Like last week, we were reading *The Great Gatsby*, and I connected it to this article I'd read about social media and how we curate false versions of ourselves online, and Mr. Patterson said it was a really insightful parallel that he'd never considered."

"That's a strength."

"I guess? But I also forgot to turn in the actual essay on time, so..."

"Ava, I'm going to ask you something important. Do you think ADHD has any positives? Any strengths? Or is it only deficits?"

Ava was quiet. "I don't know. Everyone always talks about what ADHD makes hard. I've never really thought about... strengths."

"Maybe you should."

That night, Ava googled "ADHD strengths."

The results surprised her. Article after article talked about advantages associated with ADHD:

- Creativity and out-of-the-box thinking
- Ability to hyperfocus on interesting tasks
- High energy and enthusiasm
- Resilience and problem-solving (from constantly adapting)
- Ability to think quickly in crisis situations
- Passionate intensity about interests
- Pattern recognition and connecting disparate ideas
- Entrepreneurial thinking

Ava read with growing confusion. These descriptions didn't match her experience. ADHD felt like only struggle. Where were these supposed advantages in her life?

But as she read more, something shifted. The articles weren't saying ADHD was all positive. They were saying ADHD came with both challenges AND strengths. That the same traits that caused problems in traditional environments could be assets in the right contexts.

Hyperfocus was a problem when she spent six hours on a hobby project and forgot to do homework. But it was a strength when she could dive deep into something she cared about and produce exceptional work.

Impulsivity was a problem when she blurted out answers without raising her hand. But it meant she was quick-thinking and spontaneous in good ways too willing to take creative risks, try new things, speak up when others hesitated.

Distractibility was a problem in lectures. But it meant she noticed details and connections others missed. Her mind wandered to interesting places.

Maybe ADHD wasn't just a list of deficits. Maybe it was a different way of thinking that came with both costs and benefits.

In November, Ava's art teacher, Ms. Lopez, pulled her aside after class.

"Ava, I wanted to talk to you about your portfolio for college applications."

Ava had been working on an art portfolio to submit to schools with strong art programs. She loved art it was one of the few places where her ADHD brain felt like an advantage instead of a barrier.

"Your work is exceptional," Ms. Lopez said. "Genuinely creative. You have a unique perspective. You see things differently than other students."

"Thanks."

"Have you thought about writing your essay about your art? About your creative process?"

"I was going to write about ADHD. The challenges it's caused."

Ms. Lopez tilted her head. "Your ADHD is part of why your art is so good."

"What?"

"Think about it. Your mind makes unexpected connections. You combine ideas in ways others don't. You hyperfocus when you're creating and produce incredibly detailed work. Your impulsivity means you're willing to try unconventional techniques without over-thinking. All of that is ADHD. And all of that makes you a distinctive artist."

Ava had never thought about it that way. She'd always seen her art as something she did *despite* ADHD, not *because of* it.

But Ms. Lopez was right. Her best pieces came when she let her mind wander and follow unusual associations. When she hyperfocused for hours, completely absorbed. When she impulsively tried something new without worrying if it would work.

Those were all ADHD traits. And they made her art... hers.

Over the next few weeks, Ava started paying attention to moments when her ADHD brain was actually helpful.

In debate club, when their planned argument fell apart mid-round, Ava's brain kicked into high gear. She thought quickly, pivoted strategy on the spot, came up with a new angle that saved the round. Her partner said afterward, "How do you think that fast under pressure?" Ava realized: ADHD brains are wired for novelty and quick adaptation. Crisis situations activated her in a way routine didn't.

In creative writing class, when they had to write flash fiction in thirty minutes, Ava's impulsivity was an advantage. She didn't over-think. She just wrote, following her instincts, letting the story flow. She won the class competition. Her teacher said, "Your spontaneity comes through. There's an energy to your writing that feels immediate and alive."

In her part-time job at a busy café, Adhd helped her juggle multiple orders, adapt to chaos, notice patterns in customer preferences, stay energized during rushes. Her manager said she was the best employee in high-pressure situations. Static, slow days were harder. But when things got hectic, Ava thrived.

In her friend group, her ADHD made her the idea person. "Let's try that new restaurant." "What if we went thrifting instead?" "I have a crazy idea for the school fundraiser." Her spontaneity and enthusiasm kept things interesting. Her ability to make unexpected connections meant conversations with her never felt boring.

Ava started keeping a list in her phone: *ADHD Advantages I've Actually Experienced.*

The list grew longer than she expected.

In December, Ava had a breakthrough.

Her history teacher assigned a research paper comparing two different historical periods. Most students chose obvious comparisons: World War I and World War II, or Ancient Rome and Ancient Greece.

Ava's brain made a weird connection: the fall of Blockbuster and the fall of the Roman Empire.

It sounded absurd. But the more she researched, the more parallels she found: failure to adapt to changing conditions, overconfidence in established systems, ignoring warning signs, collapse accelerated by innovation from competitors.

She wrote the paper following these unusual connections. She was nervous turning it in. What if it was too weird? Too random? What if the connections only made sense to her ADHD brain?

She got the paper back a week later. A+. Her teacher had written: *This is the most creative historical analysis I've seen in years. Your ability to draw parallels across completely different contexts shows sophisticated pattern recognition. Excellent work.*

Ava stared at the comment. "Pattern recognition." That was an ADHD strength. Her brain's tendency to make unexpected connections wasn't just random it was a cognitive skill.

By January, Ava's perspective on ADHD had fundamentally shifted.

She still struggled. The challenges were real. She still needed accommodations. Still forgot things. Still got distracted. Still found traditional school environments difficult.

But she was starting to see ADHD as more than just problems. It was a different neurological architecture that came with trade-offs. Yes, focusing in lectures was harder. But making creative connections was easier. Yes, organizing traditional tasks was challenging. But thinking divergently came naturally.

She wasn't broken. She was different. And different came with both costs and gifts.

In February, Ava finally sat down to write her college essay.

This time, instead of listing deficits, she wrote about creativity.

She described her art process how her mind wandered and made unexpected connections, how she'd combine images from a documentary she'd watched with techniques from a random article she'd read, how her hyperfocus allowed her to work for hours perfecting details.

She wrote about the Blockbuster/Roman Empire paper and how her brain naturally saw patterns across disparate contexts.

She wrote about the debate round where she'd pivoted strategy mid-competition and saved the day through quick thinking.

She wrote: *I have ADHD. For years, I saw this only as a challenge a list of things that were harder for me than for neurotypical people. But I've learned that ADHD isn't just deficits. It's a different way of thinking that comes with distinctive strengths.*

My ADHD brain makes unexpected connections. It thinks divergently when others think linearly. It thrives in novel situations and creative challenges. It can hyperfocus intensely on work I'm passionate about. These aren't compensations for ADHD they're part of what ADHD is.

Traditional educational environments aren't designed for ADHD brains. Sitting still, following linear instructions, completing routine tasks in predetermined ways these are all challenges for me. But when I'm in environments that value creativity, rapid adaptation, and unconventional thinking, my ADHD becomes an advantage.

I'm applying to your art program because I want to study in an environment that values the way my brain works. Where making unexpected connections is celebrated, not penalized. Where hyperfocus on creative work is encouraged. Where thinking differently isn't a deficit it's the whole point.

Ava read the essay over. It was honest about challenges but didn't wallow in them. It reframed ADHD as a cognitive difference with both costs and benefits. It showed self-awareness and growth.

Most importantly, it felt true. Not toxic positivity pretending

ADHD was all great. But realistic acknowledgment that ADHD came with genuine strengths she'd learned to recognize and cultivate.

In March, college acceptances started arriving.

Ava got into her top choice: a liberal arts school with a strong art program known for valuing creative thinking and unconventional approaches.

The acceptance letter included a note from the admissions officer: *Your essay about ADHD and creativity stood out to us. We value students who think differently and bring unique perspectives. We believe you'll thrive here.*

Ava cried reading it. Someone valued her ADHD brain. Saw it as an asset, not just a challenge to accommodate.

In April, Ava presented her senior art portfolio at the school art show.

One piece, titled "Different Architecture," showed two buildings side by side. One was a traditional brick building, perfectly symmetrical, organized, conventional. The other was a modern structure with unusual angles, unexpected materials, unconventional design.

Below it, she'd written: *ADHD isn't a broken version of neurotypical. It's different architecture. Both are valid. Both have strengths. Mine just looks different from traditional structures and that's okay.*

Several teachers stopped to talk to her about the piece. Her AP Psychology teacher said, "This is a sophisticated understanding of neurodiversity. Have you thought about studying neuroscience or psychology?"

Ava hadn't. But the suggestion planted a seed. Maybe she could study how different brains worked. Maybe her ADHD perspective would be valuable in understanding neurodiversity.

In May, Ava gave a presentation to the school's ADHD support group. She'd been asked to talk about preparing for college with ADHD.

"I want to talk about something that nobody really tells you," Ava started. "ADHD has strengths. Real ones. Not 'silver lining' fake positivity. Actual cognitive advantages."

She shared her list:

- Creative thinking and unusual connections
- Hyperfocus on engaging work
- Quick thinking in crisis or novel situations
- High energy and enthusiasm
- Willingness to take risks and try new approaches
- Pattern recognition across different contexts
- Resilience from constant adaptation
- Passionate intensity about interests

"These aren't things that make up for ADHD challenges," she said. "They're part of what ADHD is. The same brain wiring that makes traditional school hard can make creative work easier. The same impulsivity that gets you in trouble can make you brave enough to try things others won't. The same distractibility that hurts in lectures can help you notice details and connections others miss."

A freshman raised their hand. "But what if I don't feel like I have any strengths? What if ADHD just feels like... problems?"

"It felt like that for me too," Ava said. "For years. Because school is designed for neurotypical brains. Traditional environments punish ADHD traits and don't create spaces where ADHD strengths can show up."

"So what changed?"

"I started paying attention to moments when my ADHD brain was actually helpful. Times when I thought quickly, made creative connections, hyperfocused productively, adapted well to chaos. Those moments were always there. I just hadn't been counting them as 'ADHD' because I'd been taught that ADHD was only deficits."

Another student asked, "Are you saying ADHD is a superpower? Because that feels like toxic positivity."

"No," Ava said firmly. "ADHD is genuinely challenging. I still struggle. I still need accommodations. I'm not saying it's all great. I'm saying it's a mixed picture. There are real costs AND real benefits. And recognizing the benefits doesn't erase the costs it just makes the full picture more accurate."

On the last day of senior year, Ava cleaned out her locker.

She found old notes from freshman year, back when she'd just been diagnosed. She'd written: *I have ADHD. This explains why everything is so hard.*

She pulled out her phone and looked at the note she'd written last week: *I have ADHD. This explains why I think differently both the challenges and the strengths.*

Four years. Same diagnosis. Completely different understanding.

That summer, before leaving for college, Ava created one final art piece.

It was a split canvas. On one side, she painted the challenges of ADHD: tangled threads representing disorganization, fractured attention, scattered thoughts, time slipping away, forgotten tasks, impulsive mistakes.

On the other side, she painted the strengths: explosive bursts of creative energy, webs of unexpected connections, vibrant intensity, rapid adaptation, passionate focus, unconventional pathways.

In the center, where the two sides met, she painted herself. Not divided. Not choosing one side over the other. But existing in both spaces simultaneously. Because ADHD was both. Always both.

She titled it: *The Full Picture.*

The night before leaving for college, Ava's parents found her in her room, looking at her college acceptance letter.

"Nervous?" her dad asked.

"A little. But mostly excited."

"You've come a long way," her mom said. "Freshman year, you were so focused on everything ADHD made difficult. Now you seem... different."

"I am different. Not because my ADHD changed it didn't. But because I understand it differently now."

"How so?"

"I used to think ADHD was just a collection of problems. Things I couldn't do, ways I was broken, accommodations I needed. And those challenges are real they're still there. But I also started seeing the other side. The creative thinking, the quick adaptation, the passionate intensity. Those are part of ADHD too. They're not compensation for the challenges. They're part of the same neurological package."

Her dad nodded. "So you're not 'overcoming' your ADHD. You're learning to work with it."

"Exactly. I'm going to a college that values creative thinking. I'm studying art, which plays to my brain's strengths. I'm building a life around what my ADHD brain does well, while also having accommodations for what it doesn't. I'm not trying to become neurotypical. I'm trying to be the best version of my ADHD self."

Ava's first week of college confirmed her intuition.

Her roommate, Mei, didn't have ADHD. She was organized, focused, traditional in her thinking. She'd be a great biology major.

But when Mei got stuck on a paper about ethical implications of genetic engineering, she asked Ava for help.

"I can't think of a unique angle. Everything I come up with feels obvious."

Ava's brain immediately made connections: genetic engineering → designer babies → social media filters → construction of identity → *The Great Gatsby*.

"What if you connected it to how we already engineer our identities through social media? Like, genetic engineering is just taking that impulse to curate an ideal version of ourselves to its biological extreme?"

Mei's eyes widened. "That's brilliant. How did you think of that?"

"ADHD brain. I make weird connections."

"Can I borrow your brain for all my papers?"

Ava laughed. "Sure. And you can teach me how to keep my desk organized."

In October, Ava's art professor assigned a project: create something that represents your unique perspective.

While other students sketched and planned, Ava dove in impulsively. She hyperfocused for twelve hours straight, combining techniques she'd learned with materials she'd never used before, following associations and instincts rather than a predetermined plan.

The result was chaotic and unconventional and distinctively hers.

When she presented it, her professor said, "This is what I mean by unique perspective. You think differently. You see connections others don't. You're willing to take creative risks. These are gifts. Cultivate them."

Ava felt something settle in her chest. Not despite ADHD. Because of it.

One afternoon in November, Ava video-called with a high school friend who was struggling freshman year at a different college.

"I hate it here," her friend Jade said. "Everything is so structured. So many rules. I feel like I'm suffocating."

"What school did you choose?"

"Engineering program. Really traditional. Lots of lectures, problem sets, rigid requirements."

"That sounds tough for an ADHD brain."

"I thought I could handle it. But I'm drowning. Maybe I'm just not cut out for college."

"Or maybe you chose a program designed for neurotypical brains. Have you looked into transferring to something that fits your brain better?"

"You mean give up? Quit?"

"I mean make a strategic decision about what environment lets your brain work at its best. That's not giving up. That's self-awareness."

Jade was quiet. "You really think there are programs where ADHD is actually an advantage?"

"I'm in one. Art program. Values creative thinking, unconventional approaches, hyperfocus on passion projects. My ADHD brain thrives here. Not because I don't have challenges I still need accommodations, still struggle with some things. But the environment is designed around what brains like ours do well."

"I never thought about it that way."

"Most people don't. We're taught to see ADHD as only deficits. But it's trade-offs. Some environments punish our challenges and ignore our strengths. Other environments minimize our challenges and amplify our strengths. The goal is finding the right fit."

By winter break, Ava had settled into college life.

She'd joined the school's neurodiversity club, where she met other students with ADHD, autism, dyslexia, and various brain differences. They talked about challenges but also about strengths. About reframing neurodivergence not as broken neurotypicality but as legitimate cognitive variation.

She'd connected with a professor studying creativity and ADHD, who was excited to have an art student willing to participate in research.

She'd built a schedule that worked for her brain: intensive studio time when she could hyperfocus, movement breaks, classes clustered to reduce transition difficulties, accommodations for executive function challenges.

Most importantly, she'd stopped apologizing for her ADHD brain. Stopped trying to hide it or compensate for it or overcome it. She just worked with it.

For her final project before break, Ava created a series called "Different Doesn't Mean Deficit."

Each piece highlighted a different ADHD trait, showing both the challenge it caused in traditional contexts and the strength it provided in the right environment:

Hyperfocus: *Can't stop working on passion project, forgets to eat → Produces exceptional detailed work through sustained intense concentration*

Distractibility: *Can't follow boring lecture → Notices details and patterns others miss*

Impulsivity: *Blurts out answers without thinking → Willing to take creative risks others avoid*

Tangential thinking: *Gets off topic easily → Makes unexpected connections across different domains*

High energy: *Can't sit still in class → Brings enthusiasm and intensity to interesting work*

The series won the freshman showcase award. The judges said her work "challenges conventional narratives about neurodevelopmental differences and offers a more nuanced understanding of cognitive diversity."

Ava framed the judge's comments and hung them in her dorm room.

On the last night of fall semester, Ava updated her college essay not to submit anywhere, just for herself.

The original version she'd submitted said: *ADHD isn't just deficits. It's a different way of thinking that comes with distinctive strengths.*

Now she added: *And I'm learning to build a life where those strengths matter more than the challenges. Not by overcoming my ADHD, but by putting myself in environments where my ADHD brain thrives.*

I'll always have ADHD. I'll always need accommodations. I'll always find some things harder than neurotypical people do.

But I'll also always think creatively. Make unusual connections. Hyperfocus on work I love. Adapt quickly to novel situations. Take risks others won't.

These aren't separate from my ADHD. They're part of what ADHD is.

I'm not broken. I'm different. And different has value.

Ava closed her laptop and looked around her dorm room. Art supplies organized in visual bins. Calendar with all deadlines and alarms. Fidget tools on her desk. Accommodations paperwork filed away.

She'd built systems for her challenges. But she'd also built a life around her strengths.

Both were necessary. Both were part of having ADHD.

The next morning, heading home for break, Ava's phone buzzed. An email from a high school junior asking about her ADHD college essay.

Hi Ava, my counselor showed me your essay about ADHD strengths. I have ADHD too and I've only ever thought about it as problems. How did you figure out your strengths?

Ava typed back:

I started paying attention to moments when my ADHD brain was actually helpful instead of only noticing when it made things hard. I realized that the same traits that cause challenges in traditional environments can be advantages in the right contexts. I stopped trying to be neurotypical and started building a life around what my ADHD brain does well.

ADHD is both challenges AND strengths. Both are real. Both matter. Don't let anyone tell you it's only one or the other.

You're not broken. You're different. Figure out what your different brain does well, then build toward that.

She hit send and smiled.

Four years ago, she'd needed someone to tell her that. Now she could be that person for someone else.

The ADHD advantage wasn't that everything was easy. It was understanding that her brain came with both costs and gifts and learning to build a life where the gifts mattered.

That was enough.

———

REFLECT

Ava's story is about reframing ADHD from "only deficits" to "both challenges and strengths." If you've internalized that ADHD is just a list of problems, or if you've never considered that your ADHD brain might have genuine advantages, this story is for you.

1. **Ava initially saw ADHD as only deficits a list of everything she struggled with and nothing positive. When you think about your ADHD, do you see only problems?** What would it mean to consider that ADHD might come with both costs and benefits?

----

2. **Ava's art teacher pointed out that her creativity, unusual connections, hyperfocus, and willingness to try unconventional techniques were all ADHD traits that made her art exceptional. Have you ever considered that some of your strengths might be because of ADHD, not despite it?** What abilities or qualities might actually be connected to your ADHD?

   ----

3. **Ava discovered she thrived in high-pressure, novel situations (debate crisis, busy café shifts) while struggling with routine, static environments. Do you notice your ADHD brain performing better in certain contexts?** What situations make your ADHD traits advantages rather than obstacles?

   ----

4. **Ava's "weird" connections (Blockbuster and Roman Empire) that seemed random were actually sophisticated pattern recognition. Do you make unusual connections others don't see?** Have you been taught to suppress this or dismiss it as "off-topic" rather than recognizing it as a cognitive strength?

____

____

____

____

5. **Ava realized that traditional school environments aren't designed for ADHD brains they punish ADHD traits and don't create spaces where ADHD strengths can show up. Do you find yourself judging your abilities based on performance in environments designed for neurotypical brains?** How might your assessment of yourself change in different contexts?

____

____

____

____

6. **Ava distinguished between toxic positivity ("ADHD is a superpower!") and realistic acknowledgment (ADHD has genuine costs AND benefits). Can you hold both truths that ADHD creates real challenges AND provides real strengths?** How does this differ from pretending everything is great?

____

____

____

____

7. **Ava chose a college program that valued what her ADHD brain does well (creativity, unconventional thinking, passionate focus) while providing accommodations for challenges. Are you building toward environments that play to your strengths, or**

trying to force yourself to succeed in environments designed for different brains?

____

____

____

____

8. **By the end, Ava understood: "I'm not broken. I'm different. And different has value." Do you believe this about yourself?** What would change if you truly saw your ADHD brain as different architecture rather than broken neurotypical?

____

____

____

____

ACT

This week, identify and cultivate your ADHD strengths while maintaining realistic acknowledgment of challenges.

ADHD isn't just deficits research consistently shows it comes with genuine cognitive advantages. The same neurological differences that create challenges in traditional environments provide strengths in the right contexts. Your task is to discover what YOUR ADHD brain does well and start building toward environments where those strengths matter.

Create your "ADHD Strengths Inventory":

Start a note in your phone or journal titled "My ADHD Strengths." For one week, actively notice moments when your ADHD traits are actually helpful, not harmful. These might include:

- **Creative connections:** Times when you see relationships between ideas others miss, make unusual associations, or think "outside the box" naturally

- **Hyperfocus advantage:** When you dive deep into something you care about and produce exceptional work through sustained concentration
- **Crisis performance:** Moments when you think quickly under pressure, adapt rapidly to unexpected situations, or thrive in chaos while others freeze
- **Passionate intensity:** When your enthusiasm and energy about topics you love is contagious and drives you to learn deeply
- **Risk-taking courage:** Times when your impulsivity means you're willing to try things others won't, speak up when others stay quiet, or experiment with unconventional approaches
- **Pattern recognition:** When you notice details, spot trends, or identify connections across different domains that others overlook
- **Rapid ideation:** When you generate lots of ideas quickly, brainstorm effectively, or approach problems from multiple angles simultaneously

Each time you notice one of these moments, write it down with specific details: *"In debate, when our argument fell apart, I pivoted strategy mid-round and found a new angle that saved us ADHD quick thinking"* or *"Spent 6 hours on my art project and created my best work ADHD hyperfocus."*

After one week, review your list. You're looking for patterns which ADHD strengths show up most consistently for you? Then ask yourself:

What environments, activities, or careers would value these specific strengths? If you excel at creative connections, consider fields that reward innovative thinking (design, writing, research, entrepreneurship). If you thrive in crisis situations, consider careers with high pressure and novelty (emergency services, event planning, journalism). If you hyperfocus on passions, consider work that allows deep engagement with topics you love.

What one step can you take this month to move toward an

environment where your ADHD strengths matter more? This might mean: switching to a more creative elective, joining a club that values quick thinking, researching colleges/careers that fit your brain, talking to someone working in a field that matches your strengths, or starting a passion project that uses your hyperfocus productively.

Important reminders:

- ADHD strengths are real not compensation for deficits, but part of what ADHD neurologically is
- Recognizing strengths doesn't erase challenges both exist simultaneously
- You're not "broken neurotypical" you're differently structured, with different trade-offs
- Traditional school environments punish ADHD traits and hide ADHD strengths poor performance there doesn't define your potential
- The goal isn't to become neurotypical it's to build a life where your ADHD brain's advantages matter more than its challenges
- Different brains thrive in different environments success means finding your fit, not forcing yourself into environments designed for other brain types

CHAPTER 13
CONCLUSION: BUILDING YOUR PATH FORWARD

YOU'VE JUST READ twelve stories about teens with ADHD who learned to thrive.

Tyler discovered his struggles weren't laziness but undiagnosed ADHD masked by intelligence. Zara learned she wasn't behind she operated on a different timeline. Mason harnessed hyperfocus as a tool instead of being controlled by it. Jasmine understood emotional dysregulation as neurology, not character flaw. Jordan learned to reality-check RSD before spiraling.

Riley made an informed medication decision. Ben built ADHD-friendly organization systems. Sienna created gaps between impulse and action. Chris accommodated his body's need for movement. Maya used external frameworks to prioritize. Isaiah externalized everything his working memory couldn't hold. Ava recognized that ADHD came with genuine strengths.

Twelve different teens. Twelve different challenges. But they all learned the same fundamental truth:

They weren't broken. They were different. And different, with the right understanding and tools, could thrive.

Now it's your turn.

What You've Learned

By reading these stories, you've gained something crucial: understanding.

You understand now that:

ADHD is neurological, not behavioral. Your struggles aren't about trying harder or caring more. They're about brain differences that require different strategies and supports.

ADHD looks different for everyone. You might see yourself in three stories or in all twelve. You might have challenges the book didn't cover. That's okay ADHD is highly individual.

Strategies work, but not the same strategies for everyone. What helps Tyler might not help Mason. What works for Sienna might not work for you. Building your toolkit means trying different approaches and keeping what works.

Accommodations are equity, not advantage. Extended time, movement breaks, written instructions, recorded lectures these don't give you an unfair edge. They remove barriers neurotypical students don't face.

ADHD comes with both challenges and strengths. The same brain that makes traditional school difficult can excel at creative thinking, rapid adaptation, passionate focus, and unconventional problem-solving.

You can't become neurotypical, and you shouldn't try. Success means building a life that works for YOUR brain, not forcing your brain to work like others' brains.

Where You Are Now

Maybe you picked up this book feeling:

- Frustrated that everything is so much harder for you than for everyone else
- Exhausted from trying so hard and still falling short
- Confused about why your brain works the way it does
- Ashamed of needing accommodations or help
- Convinced that ADHD was only problems and deficits
- Alone in your struggles

If you've read these stories and worked through the Reflect and Act sections, you're in a different place now.

You understand what you're dealing with. You have language to explain your challenges. You have concrete strategies to try. You know you're not alone. You recognize that ADHD is both challenges and strengths.

Understanding changes everything.

What Comes Next

Reading this book was step one. Now comes the harder part: implementation.

Start small. Don't try to implement every strategy from every chapter simultaneously. That's overwhelming and sets you up for failure. Pick ONE challenge that's costing you most right now. Find the corresponding story. Try that ONE Act strategy for a week.

Expect imperfection. You'll forget to use strategies sometimes. You'll have setbacks. You'll have days when ADHD feels unmanageable despite all your tools. That's normal. Progress isn't linear. Keep going.

Build your personal toolkit. Some strategies from this book will work brilliantly for you. Others won't work at all. That's expected. ADHD is individual. Your toolkit will be unique to YOUR brain.

Get professional support. This book provides education and strategies, but it's not a substitute for professional help. If you don't have a therapist, psychiatrist, counselor, or ADHD coach, consider finding one. Professional support makes everything easier.

Advocate for accommodations. If you don't have formal accommodations at school, get them. Work with your counselor and parents to set up a 504 plan or IEP. Document your ADHD and specific needs. Don't try to succeed without the supports you're entitled to.

Find your people. Connect with other teens who have ADHD. Online communities, school support groups, local ADHD organizations find spaces where people understand what you're experiencing. You're not alone in this.

Educate the people around you. Share chapters from this book with parents, teachers, friends. Help them understand that ADHD isn't laziness or defiance it's neurology. The more people understand, the more support you'll receive.

Revisit this book. You don't need every strategy right now. But in six months, you might face a new challenge. Come back to the relevant chapter. This book is a resource you can return to as you grow and your needs change.

The Long View

Here's what I want you to understand about your future:

ADHD doesn't go away. You'll have ADHD your whole life. Your brain will always work differently than neurotypical brains. That's not tragic it's just reality.

But ADHD changes over time. The hyperactivity that makes you restless at 15 might channel into productive energy at 25. The impulsivity that gets you in trouble in high school might make you entrepreneurial and brave in your career. The creative thinking that's "off-topic" in class might be exactly what makes you innovative in your field.

You'll get better at managing it. Right now, you're still learning. By the time you're 25, you'll have a decade more experience building systems, identifying what works, and advocating for yourself. It gets easier not because ADHD disappears, but because you become more skilled at working with it.

You'll find environments where you thrive. High school is designed for neurotypical brains. But the world is bigger than high school. You'll find careers, communities, and contexts where your ADHD brain's strengths matter more than its challenges.

You'll meet other successful people with ADHD. Entrepreneurs, artists, athletes, scientists, teachers, doctors, engineers successful people with ADHD are everywhere. They're not successful despite ADHD. Many are successful partly because of what their ADHD brains do well.

You'll look back on this time differently. Right now, ADHD might feel like only struggle. Ten years from now, you'll see it more clearly: yes, there were challenges, but there were also strengths you didn't fully recognize yet. The creative thinking. The passionate intensity. The resilience from constantly adapting. Those weren't compensations for ADHD they were part of it.

What Success Actually Looks Like

Let's redefine success for a minute.

Success with ADHD doesn't mean:

- Never forgetting things
- Never getting distracted
- Never interrupting people
- Never struggling with tasks neurotypical people find easy
- Becoming so good at coping that nobody can tell you have ADHD

That's not success. That's hiding. That's exhausting yourself trying to pass as neurotypical.

Real success with ADHD means:

- Understanding how your brain works
- Having strategies that help you function
- Getting accommodations and support you need without shame
- Building your life around what your brain does well
- Accepting that you'll always need different tools than neurotypical people
- Thriving on your own terms, not neurotypical terms

The teens in this book are successful not because they overcame their ADHD, but because they learned to work with it.

That's what success looks like. And it's absolutely achievable.

A Few Final Truths

Before you close this book, I want to make sure you understand these things:

You are not lazy. You're working harder than most people realize just to keep up. The effort is real even when the results don't show it.

You are not stupid. ADHD has nothing to do with intelligence. Many people with ADHD are highly intelligent. Your struggles are neurological, not intellectual.

You are not broken. Your brain works differently. Different isn't defective. It's just different with different trade-offs.

You are not alone. Millions of teens have ADHD. You're part of a huge community of people who understand exactly what you're experiencing.

You are not your diagnosis. ADHD is something you have, not something you are. It's part of your neurology, but it doesn't define your worth, potential, or future.

You deserve support. You're not asking for special treatment when you request accommodations. You're asking for equity for the barriers you face to be removed so you can show what you're actually capable of.

You have value. Exactly as you are. With your ADHD brain. With your challenges and your strengths. With your different way of thinking and being. You have inherent worth that isn't contingent on productivity, success, or "overcoming" anything.

You can thrive. Not someday when you've fixed yourself. Not when you've become someone different. Right now, with ADHD, you can build a life where you thrive. It requires understanding, strategy, support, and accommodation but it's genuinely possible.

Your Next Step

Close this book and ask yourself one question:

What ONE challenge is costing me the most right now?

Is it executive dysfunction? Emotional dysregulation? Rejection sensitivity? Working memory? Impulsivity? Time management? Organization? Something else?

Identify that ONE challenge. Find the story that addresses it. Read that chapter again. Choose the ONE strategy from the Act section that feels most doable.

Then do it. This week. Not perfectly. Just try it.

That's how change happens. Not through massive overhauls or trying to fix everything at once. Through small, consistent actions that compound over time.

One strategy. One week. Then another. Then another.

Six months from now, you'll look back and realize: you've built a toolkit. You understand your brain. You have systems that work. You're thriving not despite your ADHD, but alongside it.

The Beginning, Not the End

This book ends here, but your journey with ADHD is ongoing.

You'll face new challenges. You'll discover new strengths. You'll find strategies that work and strategies that don't. You'll have good days and hard days. You'll build supports, advocate for yourself, and gradually construct a life that works for your brain.

It won't be easy. ADHD never is. But it can be good. It can be fulfilling. It can be successful on your own terms.

The teens in these stories learned to thrive. You can too.

You're not broken. You're different.

And different has value.

Now go build your path forward.

CHAPTER 14

RESOURCES

RESOURCES FOR TEENS with ADHD

Organizations & Websites:

CHADD (Children and Adults with ADHD)

Website: chadd.org

Comprehensive resource for ADHD education, support groups, and advocacy

ADDitude Magazine

Website: additudemag.com

Articles, webinars, and resources specifically for teens and adults with ADHD

Understood.org

Website: understood.org

Focuses on learning and attention issues, including ADHD

ADDA (Attention Deficit Disorder Association)

Website: add.org

Resources for teens and adults, including virtual support groups

How to ADHD (YouTube Channel)

Created by Jessica McCabe, excellent videos explaining ADHD concepts

Thriving with Richard Bass (YouTube Channel)

Created by the author of this book, videos on ADHD, gentle parenting, and neurodivergent topics

Apps & Tools:
For Time Management:

- Forest (focus timer with gamification)
- Habitica (habit tracker as RPG game)
- Todoist (simple task management)
- Google Calendar (with multiple reminder alerts)

For Organization:

- Notion (all-in-one workspace)
- Trello (visual task boards)
- SimpleMind (mind mapping)

For Focus:

- Freedom (blocks distracting websites)
- Brain.fm (music designed for focus)
- Pomodoro Timer apps

For Memory:

- Voice memos on your phone
- Google Keep (notes and lists)
- Phone camera (for visual reminders)

Finding Professional Support:
To find an ADHD specialist:

- Ask your pediatrician or school counselor for referrals
- Check Psychology Today's therapist finder (filter by ADHD specialization)
- Contact local CHADD chapters for provider recommendations

- Check if your insurance has an online provider directory

Crisis Support:
988 Suicide and Crisis Lifeline
Call or text 988
24/7 support for mental health crises
Crisis Text Line
Text HOME to 741741
24/7 text-based crisis support
National Alliance on Mental Illness (NAMI)
Website: nami.org
Call: 1-800-950-NAMI (6264)
Education, support groups, and crisis resources

Resources for Parents
Neurodivergent Teens: 12 Success Stories of Teens with ADHD and Autism who Learned to Thrive
Proven Strategies for teens with ADHD and autism
Available on Amazon
The ADHD Parenting Guide for Boys: From Toddlers to Teens
Discover How to Respond Appropriately to Different Behavioral Situations
Available on Amazon
The ADHD Parenting Guide for Girls: From Toddlers to Teens
Discover How to Respond Appropriately to Different Behavioral Situations
Available on Amazon
A Beginner's Guide on Parenting Children with ADHD
A Modern Approach to Understand and Lead your Hyperactive Child to Success
Available on Amazon
For a complete list of Richard's books on ADHD, autism, and neurodivergent support, visit amazon.com/author/richardbass

Understanding ADHD:

CHADD's National Resource Center on ADHD

Website: chadd.org/nrc

Evidence-based information for parents

ADDitude's Parent Resources

Website: additudemag.com/category/parenting-adhd-children

Articles on parenting teens with ADHD

Russell Barkley's YouTube Channel

Dr. Barkley is a leading ADHD researcher with excellent parent-focused lectures

Thriving with Richard Bass (YouTube Channel)

Created by the author of this book, videos on ADHD, gentle parenting, and neurodivergent topics for parents

School Support:

Wrightslaw

Website: wrightslaw.com

Information on special education law, IEPs, and 504 plans

Understood.org's IEP/504 Resources

Website: understood.org

Guides for navigating school accommodations

Parent Training Programs:

Look for local offerings of:

- Parent-Child Interaction Therapy (PCIT)
- Parent Management Training (PMT)
- Positive Parenting Program (Triple P)

Support for Parents:

CHADD Parent Support Groups

Find local or virtual groups through chadd.org

Facebook Groups:

- ADHD Parents Together
- Parents of Children with ADHD
- (Search for groups specific to your child's age)

Remember: Taking care of your own mental health helps you support your teen better. Consider therapy for yourself if you're feeling overwhelmed.

ABOUT THE AUTHOR

Richard Bass is a special education teacher, bestselling author, and advocate for neurodivergent children and families. With over a decade of classroom experience and more than 20 published books focused on ADHD, autism, sensory processing, and gentle parenting, Richard has helped hundreds of thousands of families worldwide better understand and support neurodivergent children.

Through his Richard Bass author brand and RBG Publishing, Richard creates practical, compassionate resources grounded in both research and real-world experience. His books have sold over 100,000 copies and are used by parents, educators, and mental health professionals across the globe.

Richard specializes in translating complex neurodevelopmental concepts into accessible, actionable strategies. His work emphasizes understanding neurodivergent children as different rather than deficient, building systems that work for how their brains actually function, and celebrating neurodiversity rather than trying to "fix" it.

When not writing or teaching, Richard can be found experimenting with new parenting approaches with his own toddler, creating content for his YouTube channel "Thriving with Richard Bass," or researching the latest developments in ADHD, autism, and child development.

Richard holds degrees in education and special education, with additional training in Cognitive Behavioral Therapy (CBT), Dialectical Behavior Therapy (DBT), and social-emotional learning approaches.

Connect with Richard:

- YouTube: Thriving with Richard Bass
- Instagram/TikTok/Facebook: @richardbassauthor
- Amazon: amazon.com/author/richardbass

Other book by Richard Bass on ADHD and Neurodivergent support?

- Neurodivergent Teens: 12 Success Stories of Teens with ADHD and Autism who Learned to Thrive
- The ADHD Parenting Guide for Boys: From Toddlers to Teens
- The ADHD Parenting Guide for Girls: From Toddlers to Teens
- A Beginner's Guide on Parenting Children with ADHD
- The Sensory Processing Handbook for Parents

For a complete list of books and resources, visit amazon.com/author/richardbass

Thank you for reading.